Always and Forever

Dara Girard

ILORI
Press Books, LLC

Other books by Dara

The Black Stockings Society
Power Play
A Gentleman's Offer
Body Chemistry
Round the Clock

Return of the Black Stockings Society
Playing for Keeps
After Hours
A Private Affair
Just One Look

Henson Series
Table for Two
Gaining Interest
Careless Rapture
Dangerous Curves
Familiar Stranger

The Clifton Sisters
The Sapphire Pendant
The Amber Stone

It Happened One Wedding
Unexpected Pleasure
Midnight Promise
Sweet Temptation

Novels
Illusive Flame
Honest Betrayal
The Daughters of Winston Barnett
Remember My Name

Dear Reader,

Welcome to another book in the *It Happened One Wedding* series where the best part of the story is after "I do."

Weddings bring many people together. Sometimes, enemies. That is the case with Bianca and Broderick two people who can't stand each other.

I wondered what would happen if that changed and I had a lot of help from the Bard.

I hope you enjoy *Always and Forever*.

All the best,
Dara

You can find out more about this series and learn about my other titles on my website www.daragirard.com

Chapter One

"**T**hey are going to ruin everything!"

"Calm yourself, my dear. There's no need to be overexcited."

"Overexcited? How can I *not* be overexcited when they are going to ruin the most important day in our daughter's life?"

Leonard Layeni dabbed his forehead with a handkerchief although he was not hot or sweating. He sighed, not knowing what else to say to his wife. They sat in the living room of the penthouse suite in the luxury hotel they owned, the cool granite floors keeping the spacious surroundings cool against the tropical spring heat spreading across the city of Lagos.

Their large complex stood tall and proud as a sanctuary against the hustle and bustle of a city known for lavish weddings, mega churches and overpopulation. Garden Paradise Hotel and Suites was designed to help travelers toss their cares and fears away and find rest and relaxation. Not a car horn could be heard once someone passed through their large glass doors.

However, he still wished he were somewhere else. Preferably in the garden of his other house-one of three they owned— outside the city where his trees were heavy with the bright red *ishin*, better known as *ackee* elsewhere, some seeming to peer down at him with split open mouths revealing three glassy black seeds. He could just smell the scent of thyme and curry, and the sound of a sizzling pan as their chef mixed the ripe *ishin* in her version of Nigerian fried rice, which she'd serve with thinly sliced sweet plantain.

But there was nothing sweet about the situation in which they now found themselves. He cast a nervous glance at his wife once more, wishing he had the words to remove the angry expression on her face. They'd been married for nearly thirty years and she was usually in a good mood. She'd never had a girlish face or figure—everything about her was round from the shape of her eyes to the breadth of her hips—but he'd always liked the look of a well-fed woman with a head on her shoulders.

She sat on the lush maroon colored couch across from him, poised like royalty, in her fashionable ankara print dress—the swirling blue and lavender color accenting her brown skin and matching her high heels. But although her skin had a rosy tint that made her brown eyes sparkle, the curl of her lip held the contempt of a queen ready to send someone to the gallows.

Esther Eunice Layeni had come from humble beginnings selling fish and palm oil in the market before she turned that simple start into an international business exporting fish, palm oil and native spices to the Americas,

Europe and Asia. His family hadn't been impressed at first; they'd been part of the Yoruba elite for generations and had no interest in a market woman who'd 'gotten lucky'. But he'd fallen in love quickly and had been the happiest man around when she agreed to be his bride.

Together, their wealth increased as did their family, although not at the pace they had hoped for. Aside from her business, his wife had the most pride in the raising of their daughter Harmony. A joy for both of them after they'd lost another daughter when she was only ten months old. No other children followed.

Leonard looked at the other figure in the room, seated in an armchair to his right. He was an old friend of his father and was respectfully referred to as "Papa Bola". While Leonard's wife carried herself like a queen, there was true royalty in Papa Bola's bloodline and he held himself with the easy arrogance of a man who'd only known privilege. He was a man of few words, keen eyes and skin as smooth and dark as a lake at night; a businessman who worked as a consultant for the family's construction division of their empire. Leonard folded his handkerchief and nodded towards the older man with the deepest respect eager to hear what he had to say. "Your thoughts are most welcome for we are at a loss."

Papa Bola tugged on his neatly trimmed white beard and shrugged.

Leonard silently groaned. He'd hoped Papa Bola would have said something to ease his wife's fears. He cleared his throat then addressed his wife again. "I'm sure it will be better tomorrow."

A lot was at stake. They'd reserved the two top floors of the hotel for their guests who were arriving from all corners of the globe and all the preparations for the grand event were already underway. They had spared no expense from the imported designer wedding dress to the grand reception hall. He'd already reconfirmed the arrival times with the vendors. He'd hired the best florist in Lagos to decorate the church and reception with enormous purple, white and pink roses, delegated a trusted friend to be in charge of securing all the wedding gifts (especially the ones that came in envelopes and had a way of 'disappearing') and left the rest of the minor details (such as who would help Harmony with her dress, or carry her personal things such as her purse) to his wife.

But as he looked at her now, he wondered if leaving any detail to her had been a mistake.

"It won't be better tomorrow," Esther said in a bitter voice. "We have to do something immediately or they are going to ruin my daughter's wedding."

"I don't think the groom will be too pleased either," Leonard said in a laconic tone.

Esther ignored him. "She upstaged her at the engagement party." She slapped her thigh then pointed at her husband. "Did you see that?"

The engagement party incident had occurred several months ago in London, but was still fresh in their minds. "It was hard to miss."

"How your sister, God rest her soul, could have raised such a girl I don't know. No man will want to marry a girl whose tongue should be removed from her mouth."

"Bianca is just young and full of ideas," Leonard said, trying to be diplomatic rather than defensive. His niece had endured a lot after her mother's untimely passing when she was nineteen. Five years before she'd had to help her mother through the death of her father who'd died in a plane crash with his mistress.

After hearing about the death of his sister, Leonard had flown to the States to make sure his niece's university education and lodgings were taken care of. And he promised her a position in one of his businesses. But, like his sister, Bianca was polite but determined to make her own way, which she did by becoming a sought after kitchen designer, although he still didn't quite understand what that kind of career entailed.

Their quiet, solitary daughter Harmony, however, saw Bianca, who was seven years older, as her hero. From her days in boarding school, Harmony kept in contact with Bianca and quickly the two cousins were as close as sisters and the bond between them seemed to grow stronger as the years passed, to his wife's annoyance.

"The wedding is tomorrow," Esther said. "I can't let my daughter's special day be usurped by that opinionated chit."

"I am sure—"

"You can be sure of nothing when it comes to Bianca. Nothing." She cut the air with her hand, making her words definitive. "If I could keep her from the wedding I would."

Leonard sent her a hard look. "You would not."

"Yes, I would."

He held her gaze. "No," he said softly but firmly. "You would not."

She lowered her gaze in deference, but he wasn't quite sure she meant it. "No, I would not."

"Because she is family," he said, in case she had forgotten the importance of that role.

Esther lifted her gaze. "You don't have to remind me of that."

"And most times you like her, and Harmony adores her."

"You don't have to remind me of that either."

"And what happened wasn't entirely her fault."

His wife stiffened, for a brief moment allowing him to be correct. "Yes, but if she could learn to curb her temper and opinions it would have been such a pleasant evening. But this is what you get for raising a girl in the States."

"Bianca thought Broderick was boasting," Leonard said, reminding her why the discord between the two had started.

"Men were born to boast and he has plenty of reasons to." She clasped her hands together, her eyes shining as if he were standing before her holding all the awards he'd won and listing all the international acclaim he'd managed to achieve as a photojournalist. "What a remarkable young man and handsome too. Too bad…"

She stopped, but Leonard silently filled in her sentence, for a moment feeling a twinge of pain. *Too bad we don't have another daughter.* That was true, but he didn't want to focus on something that could never be changed. "Bianca is just as accomplished," he said.

"I suppose," Esther said unimpressed. Her lack of interest did not surprise him. She rarely stepped into a kitchen anymore and could not understand its appeal.

"They are two good people."

"But the moment they are together things become rotten. How could they both be in the wedding party? We have to do something."

"They make a rather remarkable pair, don't you think?" Papa Bola said in a low voice.

They both looked at him surprised.

"Haven't you noticed?" he said when they looked at him with a blank stare. "Broderick is just as opinionated and obstinate as Bianca but they are both able to rally words in a manner I find very amusing."

Esther shook her head. "If they weren't in public there would be blood. They could never get on."

"I disagree. Both are attractive and intelligent."

"That's a good description of many young people," Leonard said, making his disagreement known yet still with a note of respect. "That doesn't mean anything."

His wife gripped her hands together, an intense look crossing her features. "But he's thinking of something. What is it, sah?"

Papa Bola smoothed down his beard. "An experiment of sorts that may also solve your problems."

Leonard frowned feeling suddenly uneasy. Like many with power, at times Papa Bola could be too fond of toying with people's lives. "I don't think—"

His wife waved his words away. "It's rude to interrupt," she said unaware that she was doing exactly that to him. "Let the man speak."

Leonard gripped his handkerchief in his fist. "You'd boil poor Bianca in oil if that assured your daughter the perfect wedding day."

"Don't exaggerate. However, I will go to whatever lengths are necessary to make sure that the day is perfect for *our* daughter." She turned to Papa Bola. "So what can we do, sah?"

"It will take some planning and we will need some help from people you trust."

They had more than enough staff to do what they wanted, however, Leonard still felt uneasy. "Perhaps—"

"Whatever you say," his wife cut in, her eyes bright with eagerness. "Just tell us what to do."

Leonard sighed in defeat as Papa Bola leaned forward and told them his plan.

Chapter Two

It was only her second day in Nigeria and her life was already a disaster. Bianca Olade hid behind the large shrub in the hotel courtyard, wondering how her day had gone so wrong. Yesterday, she'd endured a long flight from Washington DC to Amsterdam then Lagos, encountered congested roads with trucks belching black diesel fuel, an hour long traffic jam, where a police officer with a machine gun, angrily waved the butt of his gun at about thirty goats bleating on top of a pickup truck as if they were the cause of the delay.

When she'd finally arrived at her uncle's hotel on Victoria Island, she'd been whisked into a cool paradise located in the heart of the city, her every need immediately attended to. In her hotel room, which afforded her a view of the sea, she'd freshened up and spoken with her family and enjoyed a delicious dinner of *asaro*, yam porridge.

She'd made a minor gaff when seeing Papa Bola with her uncle in the hallway. She'd greeted him with a simple half-dip, but her Uncle Leonard's hard look of censure forced her to dip to her knees, giving Papa Bola the proper respect. Aside from that, the day had been pleasant and she'd gone to bed with little on her mind.

This morning she'd changed into a pale magenta designer dress her mother would have thought frivolous but made her feel beautiful. It was from a new Nigerian designer based in South Africa, and was a limited edition her friend had managed to get for her. It was made of a flimsy, gossamer fabric that moved with her curvy body.

She'd gone to the courtyard in her new outfit proudly flouncing around the manicured greenery, enjoying the sea breeze, taking pleasure at the looks and whispers that followed her, imagining what everyone must be thinking about her dress. Few items suited her without making her appear cuddly. She'd been called 'cute' on more than one occasion when she'd hoped to appear 'striking'. This outfit made her feel sexy and now she had the proof too.

She'd turned heads before—once or twice—but not like this, and after her recent breakup she'd needed the ego boost. It was only when she sat down on one of the benches and felt the cool concrete against her thighs that she realized what everyone had been looking at.

She'd somehow torn the back of her skirt and left her rear end exposed. She quickly darted behind a bush wondering how best to get back to her room. The gash was too wide to close by pulling the two ends together. And she'd left her cell phone in her room; otherwise she would have called for assistance. She tried to catch the eye of a passing hotel porter, but he didn't see her.

"What are you doing?"

She softly swore; dread threatening to stop her heart. She knew that arrogant, condescending male voice. It had been the voice she'd been dreading to hear the entire flight. She squeezed her eyes shut silently wishing him away. She was in hell and the devil had come to join her.

"Bianca?" he said when she didn't reply.

I'm ignoring you, you stupid man. Go away! She inwardly groaned, hoping if she stayed still and remained silent he would get the hint and leave. Of all the people to find her in this predicament, why did it have to be him? The one man she loathed. Despised. Hated.

"You look upset. I just thought you might need some help," he said.

She opened her eyes, but didn't lift her head. Dear God had he seen it all? Yes, she needed help. But not from him. Anyone but him. Please let the world come to an end first. "Let me borrow your phone."

"I don't have it with me."

How could he not have his cell phone? "Why not?"

"Where's yours?"

He had her there. "Then let me borrow your jacket," she said quickly, her impatience growing.

"I'm not wearing a jacket."

She glanced up and saw he was right. He wore khakis and a blue short sleeved shirt. He was completely useless to her. She sighed. At least if his shirt had had long sleeves she could have wrapped it around her waist. That's if he would have even let her borrow his shirt in the first place. She didn't think he had a gallant bone in his body. Broderick Radford, by all accounts, was an attractive man with light skin, broad shoulders and mischievous brown eyes. A man so vain he would kiss his shadow if he could.

"What's wrong?" he asked.

If he had to ask, then he didn't know yet. That was good. "Can you get me a robe?"

"Why?"

"Or even a towel?"

He folded his arms.

She narrowed her eyes and curled her lip. "I hate you."

He nodded, a slow smile touching his lips. "I know."

He waited.

She waited.

He waited some more.

Bianca finally rolled her eyes. The morning sun wasn't hot, but she still felt as if her skin was on fire. It was no use delaying the inevitable. "Promise not to laugh."

He shook his head. "You know I can't promise you that." He held up a hand. "But I'll try to be supportive after I get whatever it is I'm not supposed to laugh about out of my system."

Bianca sighed, anxiously looking around for help somewhere else, but no one else was in sight. She reluctantly returned her gaze to his face and said in a flat tone, "I tore my skirt."

He shrugged. "So what?"

She turned to show him the damage. "You tell me." When she turned back to him she couldn't read his expression. "It's bad, isn't it?"

He bit his lip, his eyes dancing with merriment.

Her face burned from both anger and embarrassment. "Go ahead and laugh."

He shook his head but his lip trembled. "If I start I won't stop."

She sighed. "Go away."

"How…how did you do that?"

Bianca threw up her hands in dismay. "I don't know! I didn't even hear it tear."

"That's no surprise. It looks as if it were made out of tissue paper."

"This is—"

"Wait. You didn't hear it tear?"

"No, and—"

His brows shot up. "You mean you were walking around like this and didn't even know?"

"Yes," she said through tight teeth. "Now get a porter for me or someone else at the hotel."

He looked around. "There aren't any present right now," he said, his words slowing to a crawl when he noticed an attractive, long legged woman in a short orange skirt. She caught his eye and smiled. He winked in return.

"You're into blondes now?" Bianca said in a dry tone, looking at the honey skinned beauty whose hair (dyed?) fell pass her shoulders in tight waves.

"I'm into everything."

Bianca pushed him away. "Just go. You disgust me."

"Feeling jealous are we?"

"Only if that feeling includes nausea."

He spun her towards the hotel. "Come on. I'll walk you to your room."

The man was vain and dense. She turned back to him appalled. "I can't let anyone see me like this."

He spun her around again. "I'll be behind you," he said, walking up close enough for them to touch. "No one will see."

It was one solution and she wasn't in the mood to argue. "Just stay close and in step."

He mimicked an army salute. "Yes, ma'am."

To her surprise and pleasure they easily walked in unison, his step matching hers. It would all work out.

"Did you have a good flight?" Broderick asked after a few moments. "Was your broom comfortable?"

Her pleasure faded. If she hadn't needed his help, she would have jabbed him with her elbow. "Probably more comfortable than the pet carrier you came in."

They were a few feet from the hotel entrance when he said, "I think I see part of your skirt on a—"

"Leave it. I'll get it later."

"But—"

"Just keep walking," she demanded. "I don't want anyone to see me like this."

Their pace quickened once they reached the hotel lobby were the sound of voices—German, Igbo, Yoruba, English—mingled with the sound of wheels from suitcase-laden luggage carts as they made their way across the polished floors.

They were a few feet from the elevators. Bianca smiled. Freedom was in sight. Then someone called his name.

Chapter Three

"**B**roderick!"

Bianca inwardly screamed. *Oh no!* She knew that voice. "Pretend you didn't hear her," she warned him, picking up her pace even more.

"Broderick?"

"I can't ignore her," he said.

"Try." Bianca pounded the elevator button, begging for the doors to open and end this nightmare.

"Broderick!"

"Don't turn."

"She's your aunt."

"I know that." Aunt Ursula was a woman hard to ignore. Nor was she known for her decorum. Presently she was calling out to them as if they were in an outside market. People were starting to look.

"I'll pay you," Bianca said feeling desperate.

"You couldn't pay me enough to be rude to her. I wasn't brought up that way."

Damn the man for having manners at the most inopportune moments.

Broderick turned around and gave Aunt Ursula the proper greeting while Bianca stayed put so that their backs were against each other.

"This is a surprise," Aunt Ursula said. "Margaret was just asking about you."

"It will be a pleasure to see her again," Broderick said.

"Do you want to introduce me to your friend?"

Bianca sighed, briefly hung her head then sidled her way around him until she faced her aunt. "There's no need."

She looked at her niece in surprise, an expression that didn't come easily to her. Ursula was a woman known to keeping her emotions to herself most times. She was a lean figured woman whose booming voice belied her slender frame. "I didn't think I'd find the two of you together."

"We're not together," Bianca said quickly, the thought making her shudder.

"Heaven forbid," Broderick added.

"But you were walking so fast."

Bianca sighed feeling weary. "It's because I tore—"

Broderick wrapped his arm around her waist, gripping her closer. "We're in a hurry."

She stared up at him in shock then looked at her aunt. "No, I—"

"So we'll leave you now," he said expertly turning them around and forcing Bianca to face the elevators. "What room is Margaret in?"

Aunt Ursula gave him the number.

He pushed the elevator button. To Bianca's annoyance the doors opened as if by magic. "I'll look forward to treating you two. Excuse us." He forced them into the elevator then turned to face Aunt Ursula and waved good-bye. "*Odaro.*"

"Aunty wait," Bianca said.

The doors closed.

She glared up at him. "Why wouldn't you let me tell her what happened? She could have helped me."

"I know," he said with a grin. "I didn't want the fun to end."

"I can't believe my cousin Margaret fancies you. You have all the charm of a squashed toad."

He nodded. "And you have all the grace of a bloated walrus."

"I will get you back for this."

"I'd like to see you try. Unfortunately, I don't plan to split my trousers any time soon."

"You can let go now."

"Someone could still come in."

"I don't care. I'm struggling hard not to be sick."

He clicked his tongue in pity. "Haven't been with a man that long?"

"Let go."

"I'm trying to protect your honor."

"You don't have a bone of chivalry in your body. I'll just stand against the wall."

"I don't mind."

"Isn't this uncomfortable?"

"No." He glanced down, his voice dropping with the action. "I like the view from here."

She shot him a look over her shoulder. "Don't look down."

"I never pictured you wearing bright pink."

"I told you not to look."

"I'm saying this from memory."

"No, you're not."

"No," he said, laughter in his voice. "I'm not. I am surprised though. I thought you'd be wearing a chastity belt. Since your cousin seems to have the same idea."

"There is nothing wrong with waiting for marriage."

"There's nothing wrong with sampling the meal either, especially if you've already placed your order."

"I would think that a relationship would be a little more long lasting than a meal."

"Some."

"Besides, Harmony is worth the wait."

"She seems sweet enough," he allowed.

"And I believe that Claude is marrying her for more than one reason."

"True. I just don't understand why there has to be such a big show of it."

"It's important to her and her family. At least she's not expecting him to be a virgin too."

"I doubt she'd find a husband if that was one of the requirements."

"In some cultures the men—"

"Are married by the age of twenty-two for a reason."

"Not every woman wants to be just a good time."

"No, not every woman, but enough to keep me happy," he said with a smile in his voice.

"For years to come."

"Yes."

"Which is a relief," Bianca said sounding bored. "No sensible woman would waste her time with you."

"Her time with me wouldn't be a waste."

The elevator doors opened. They stepped out together and headed down the quiet hall where a young hotel maid, with dark skin and lips as red as a pomegranate, was pushing her cart stacked high with cleaning materials. She smiled and nodded her head at them in greeting.

"I'll expect another song later, Miss Lovely," Broderick said to the maid.

She covered her mouth in embarrassed pleasure and nodded.

"I overheard her singing yesterday," Broderick explained to Bianca. "She has a beautiful voice. She told me she performs with her brother."

"I didn't ask."

"Oh, that's right. I forgot. People like her are invisible to people like you."

"If she'd been a 'he' I doubt you'd notice her either," Bianca shot back. She stopped in front of one of the doors.

"This is my room." She stepped inside then turned to him. "Thanks for your help."

Broderick rested against the doorframe. "Aren't you going to invite me in?"

She closed the door in his face.

Chapter Four

Bianca tore off her dress, bundled it into a ball then stomped on it. She'd never wear that designer again. *How humiliating!* She quickly changed into a pair of jeans and a loose dark orange and white blouse, hoping to look as insignificant as possible. She didn't want to turn heads for the remainder of the trip—maybe ever.

She lay on her bed and briefly considered jumping into the shower since she could still feel the pressure of Broderick's arm around her waist. Ugh! To think she'd been so close to him. And how could a man almost consistently smell like coconut and bananas as if he were a tropical island? The image suited him since his skin was the color of hot sand, but he was no place she'd ever want to visit.

Bianca sat up and took off her blouse—irritated that she was even thinking about Broderick—and selected a more subdued dark blue colored one. If she'd had something in black she would have worn it because she definitely felt in mourning. How could she face him again? He'd be smirking at her the rest of the day (she glanced at her watch and groaned. She had two hours before it was even noon and the day was starting to feel like forever) and likely through the wedding. She pounded the bed with her fists. *It wasn't fair!*

She closed her eyes, took a deep steadying breath, then jumped to her feet. She'd weather this. She wouldn't let this embarrassing situation get to her. The first and last time she'd let Broderick rattle her was three years ago. She'd first met him one spring day at Papa Bola's seventieth birthday party, which was hosted in a rented medieval Italian castle where she remembered the cypress lined road, rolling green hills, and indulging in the scent and taste of Sicilian mandarins, which were as sweet as candy. The fairy tale atmosphere had put her in a romantic mood.

Bianca fell back on the bed and sighed at the memory. The brief introduction, with the man who would become her nemesis, had let her know what was very clear to everyone else. He was an attractive, entertaining man who knew how to make others feel at ease. To her shame, and horror, she'd been a little smitten when he'd smiled at her.

Then he'd ignored her.

Twice.

The first time she'd found him alone, which wasn't easy since people seemed to be drawn to him like thirsty animals to a lake, she'd walked up behind him and said, "Have you ever been to Naples?" She'd overheard him discussing the different areas of Italy he'd been to and his love of pizza. She knew eating pizza in Naples would be a treat for him. Instead of turning around, or acknowledging her, he'd waved at one of his friends and walked away.

She'd been stunned by his rudeness, but then explained it away thinking she may not have spoken loud enough. The large ballroom was crowded and various conversations buzzed around them so it was possible. With that conclusion in mind she approached him again with renewed boldness when she saw him talking with a group.

At first she quietly listened as he told one of his harrowing tales of danger and escape with dramatic flair that kept her, and everyone else in the group, on edge, then when he'd finished and his audience had gone, she said, a little louder to make sure he would hear her, "That must have been horrible. Tell me more."

But instead of replying, he'd turned around, looked straight at her for one brief moment then just walked away. Again! Just walked off as if she hadn't spoken. As if she didn't exist. He'd left her standing there feeling like a fool.

He'd made it clear (twice!) that she wasn't attractive enough for him to notice and her heart had turned from hurt to hate and she never looked back.

Her recent ex-boyfriend, Demarco, had made her feel the same. She'd made the same foolish error of falling for a man's charm and looks instead of something more substantial. They'd had six good months together. At least she'd thought they were good until he'd told her that he didn't think they would work.

He'd told her this while they were sitting in the packed Nationals stadium located along the Anacostia River in

Washington DC with the home team losing badly. All the bases were loaded and a rookie was headed to the bat. The air smelled of hot dogs and cigarettes from a group of rowdy college age kids who seemed to have inhaled a pack each.

Demarco rubbed his hands on his jeans and quietly said, "It's not going to work."

"Shh," Bianca said, her eyes focused on the field, the large pretzel she'd ordered still uneaten in her hands. "Of course it will work. There's still enough time left."

"I don't mean the game. I mean us."

She stared at him with her pretzel halfway to her mouth. She thought baseball was boring but at least she was trying. It was his birthday and she'd bought the tickets for him. "I didn't mean to fall asleep last time. I promise I'll stay awake."

His eyes looked sad. He wore the expression well. It was one of the reasons she'd fallen for him. "It's not that."

"And I won't force you to another gallery opening. I know you hate them."

He shook his head looking a little more dejected as if she'd just popped his favorite balloon. "It's not that either."

Bianca's heart began to pound as she came to fully real- ize the situation. *Please don't breakup with me here in front of all these people.* She noticed one of the college kids nudging his friend. She half expected her face to show up on the large LED screen with the word 'loser' over her head. Who breaks up with someone on their birthday? "Can't we talk about this later?"

"I'm sorry. I don't mean to hurt you."

She set her pretzel down, her appetite gone. "But you will anyway."

"The truth is…you scare me."

"How could I scare you?"

"You're a little bit too much."

"Too much what?"

He shrugged. "I don't know." He waved his hands. "It's really not about you. It's about me."

She resisted the urge to slap the side of his face with her mustard covered pretzel. She wanted to stop him before he gave her that paltry, insulting breakup speech. "I'm too much what?" she demanded. "Be specific."

He shook his head his eyes filled with regret. "You don't want to hear it."

Don't be a coward now, you started this. "Yes, I do."

"You're too much…you."

No, she didn't want to hear that. She didn't even understand it. But within minutes he gave her the specifics that she'd asked for.

He didn't like her brash style, her bold manner. He compared her to a tornado. "You're nice and all," he said, trying to soften his words with a compliment. The effort didn't work. His words still felt like poisoned darts. "But you're too much for a guy to take. I mean, you are cute and all and that fooled me at first…"

Fooled you? You think I fooled you?

"…but you're not at all the way you look. If you could tone it down a bit maybe…"

Bianca didn't listen to the rest because there was nothing she could do. There was nothing to 'tone down'. This was who she was and she wasn't going to change. Could she help it that she had the heart of a grizzly in the body of a teddy bear? She saw herself as a warrior with scars and he wanted an angel.

She'd be nobody's angel. Nobody's cuddly toy. She'd never change for anyone. But his words burned her heart more than she wanted to admit.

A month after their breakup, she'd spotted him in a restaurant with a woman who seemed to be his ideal. The kind of woman who laughed prettily at his jokes and who let him order for her.

She remembered how shocked he'd been on their first date when she'd ordered for herself and even gave him several suggestions. But the sight of him with his new love still hurt, reminding her that she could never be that woman. She was too aware that a woman had to be strong or men, like her father, could destroy them. His lies and infidelity had devastated her mother.

She'd made a mistake, wasting her feelings on the wrong man. Men like Broderick and Demarco could go to hell. If they were too weak to take her strength, she'd crush them and enjoy it. She wouldn't be one of those females who withered under the weight of a man's ego. She'd been hurt once too many. Now she'd be in charge.

Bianca stood and went to her window. She hoped her cousin, Harmony, had found a man who deserved her. Harmony was the kind of woman Demarco would like. She didn't envy her cousin's sweet, serious ways, she loved her too much to feel that way, but she did worry sometimes. At twenty-three, Harmony was so trusting and pure in a world where few people were. She hoped Claude was everything he appeared to be and was a man who would stay true. Harmony deserved a man who didn't just see her family's fortune. Or think about how good she looked on his arm.

This wedding not only held her cousin's hopes and dreams, but her own. She knew she'd never have her own wedding day, because there was no man alive who was her true equal. No man who she would ever trust with her heart. So tomorrow, for one brief moment, she would live through her cousin and believe in true love and the joining of lives together until death, knowing it was a dream out of her reach.

Bianca left her room feeling restless. She walked to the lounge area where she saw a good looking older man with a woman young enough to be his granddaughter taking pictures of themselves. She stopped when she saw Broderick with the same long legged blonde from before and two of her friends. She watched him remove something from his pocket and noticed a piece of paper fall out. She thought to leave it, but then decided to say something, since no one else seemed to notice. Her uncle took pride in keeping his hotel clean and she couldn't have this jerk littering it because he was too busy trying to get laid.

Bianca picked the paper up, not surprised to see that it was money—even in Italy her uncle had chided him on handling his money carelessly when he'd spent more than he should have at a local shop that had been struggling for business—then said, "If you want to throw money around, do so in private."

When he didn't turn, she felt her temper snap. He was going to ignore her a third time? She opened her mouth to say it a little louder when one of the women, with dark brows and purple lipstick, nodded towards her. Broderick looked behind him and jumped when he saw her. As if she were a troll that had frightened him. He quickly recovered himself, measured the length of her in one swift glance and said, "What? No skirt?"

Bianca scowled and held out the money. "You dropped this."

"It's not much, you can keep it."

"I don't need the charity." She shoved the money back in his trouser pocket.

Broderick looked at the women and said with a note of apology, "She's been trying to get in my trousers for years."

Bianca thought of replying with something rude, but thought better of it and spun away. She stopped when she saw Claude resting against the wall laughing. He matched his friend in good looks but their similarities ended there. Claude had a more trusting nature and was jovial and carefree, which Bianca hoped would balance her cousin's more serious demeanor.

Right now Bianca found him irritating. "You think this is funny?"

He nodded, unfazed by her sour tone. "You really scared him."

There was that word again. Scared. Were men really that easily frightened? She began to walk past him and muttered, "That's what you get for trying to be helpful."

"He would have thanked you, but he was embarrassed."

She stopped and looked at him. "Embarrassed?"

Claude nodded. "Because you scared him."

She rolled her eyes. "How in the world did I scare him?"

"He didn't know you were there."

"Because he was ignoring me."

"No, because he didn't hear you." He motioned her closer, when she leaned in he said, "It's not something Broderick likes known, but he's deaf in his right ear. If he's in a crowd or people are talking to him and you stand behind him on that side he can't hear you. If you're beside him it's only marginally better."

"Deaf? Since childhood?"

Claude shook his head, his expression growing serious. "No. On one of his travels about five years ago, he'd gotten kidnapped by a rebel group that tortured him. I won't tell you where it happened because it's not something he likes to talk about so don't bring it up."

"You're sure he's not pretending?"

"I'm sure," Claude said, all humor gone from his voice and eyes. "I wouldn't joke about something like that."

"But you were laughing," Bianca said confused.

"Only because of his pride. He likes to pretend that people not knowing about his deafness doesn't matter, but moments like this remind him that it does. I've tried to get him to stop being ashamed, but he won't listen to me."

"I don't believe it."

Claude walked towards Broderick. "Here, I'll show you."

She grabbed his arm, stopping him. "No, it's okay," she said as she let his words sink in. "I didn't mean 'I don't believe it' literally, it was just a figure of speech." She studied the back of Broderick's head as he laughed with the women. He hadn't heard her? All those years ago he hadn't been ignoring her? He just hadn't heard her?

She mentally shook her head. That was cold comfort now. She knew the kind of man he truly was. *She's been trying to get in my trousers for years.* The smug bastard.

But she now had ammunition. He couldn't use the courtyard incident against her; she had something new in her arsenal against him.

Be careful how you tease me Broderick, you may be in for a surprise.

Chapter Five

argaret would be next.

Ursula tightened the skirt of her daughter's outfit with dreams of the beautiful white gown her daughter would wear on her wedding day.

"Ow!" Margaret cried. "Mum, you're pulling too tight. I told you I can do this myself."

"Not like this," Ursula said, loosening the fabric a bit as she returned her thoughts to the wax print skirt she'd bought for her daughter. "This is important. When you see him you must be at your best."

Although there was really no need to say so. Margaret always looked her best. She was a natural beauty—with cocoa skin and full lips—and in the next two days that beauty would be rewarded. Ursula planned to see her daughter engaged and then married within the year.

Seeing Broderick again made Ursula's plan feel even more urgent and essential. She didn't want her daughter in the arms of a wealthy older man as many of Margaret's peers seemed apt to do, proudly displaying their 'sugar babies' status with fine clothes and paid for flats; nor did she want her daughter as a married man's mistress, although she'd received plenty of offers. No, she wanted to see her daughter as a bride.

And Broderick would be the perfect groom. She'd met him on two occasions already and he was always pleasant and warm. She had to snag a man like him quickly. Seeing him with Bianca this morning had been worrying. Although they were usually on the verge of scratching each other's faces, she didn't put it past Bianca having an agenda. Single women could be very conniving. There was no time to waste.

Ursula looked at her daughter, her mood turning bitter. She shouldn't have been fixing her daughter up anyway. She should have been catering Harmony's reception instead of attending it.

"But we want you to just enjoy yourself," her sister, Esther, had told her when Ursula had broached the subject.

Ursula didn't believe a word of it. Her sister was such a liar. Did Esther really think she'd believe that she hadn't used Ursula's catering company because she wanted her to just be a guest? What would have been the harm in letting her cater her own niece's wedding? Did she think her food was too regional? Not posh enough?

Ursula prided herself on her business. She was one of the best around, although word of that fact hadn't spread fast or far enough in the five years of their existence. Catering Harmony's wedding would have given her business the extra cash it needed, plus some publicity. What a grand flyer she could have created if Esther had let her. She could just imagine how she would have positioned the bride and groom, with wide smiles on their faces, behind her buffet table displaying a mix of Western and African fare.

She could also see the faces of their distinguished guests. Senator Adetokunbo would have loved her *amala and ewedu soup,* soon her phone wouldn't stop ringing.

But her cunning sister had stolen that possible glory from her just as she'd stolen their father's love years ago when he'd married Esther's mother. Ursula remembered her mother being usurped by her father's third wife.

Ursula looked around the hotel room in contempt. Even the room she'd put her and Margaret in was just to show how well she'd done for herself. Did Esther really need to put them in one of the grand suites that gave them a panoramic view of the city? Did she really need to see the enormous crystal vase filled with fresh flowers sparkling on the dining table?

Soon luxury would no longer be a hand me down, but hers for the taking. Margaret's marriage would see to that. Harmony wasn't the only one who had caught the eye of an eligible gentleman. Broderick would also help elevate their family status. Although he had roots in the Caribbean, his family was well established in America. He could take Margaret, and her, far away from here, so it was Margaret's job to convince him of how perfect she was for him. She only had two days-today and tomorrow—to put her plan into action. People made matches at weddings all the time and this wedding would be the key to their success.

Chapter Six

Harmony stared at her mother, as she sat across from her in the sitting room, not entirely sure her mother was sane. "I understand that putting Broderick and Bianca together in the wedding party was probably a bad idea, but I'm not sure Papa Bola's idea is…is—"

"It's perfect," Esther said, leaving little room for argument. She'd invited her daughter to the suite to tell her of their plans, the scent of toasted, buttered English teacakes and black tea lingered in the air. "Your father should be speaking to Claude now. Just do as we ask." She gripped her hands together, pleading. "Please. We don't have much time. I've taken care of everything else. The assembling of the welcome baskets for the guests is being done this instant by a hired staff. You're already packed for your honeymoon. But this plan won't work without you."

"Are you sure it will work at all?"

"It will. Papa Bola is a wise man. You're too cautious like your father. This is not a time to ponder. We must act."

"Isn't there something else we can do?"

"Un-invite one of them."

Harmony frowned. "That's not possible and you know it. They've both travelled a long distance to be here. Bianca is my cousin and Broderick is Claude's best friend and Papa Bola's holds him in high esteem too. We couldn't not invite one of them."

"Yes, you can."

"Mum, that's not possible."

"So this is our only option. I will not let what happened at the engagement party happen again."

Harmony suppressed a giggle. The London party had been a wonderfully awful disaster with Bianca and Broderick hurling insults throughout the evening while the other guests' heads turned left to right, watching the pair as if they were at a tennis match.

"It's not funny," Esther said, catching her daughter's expression.

Harmony covered her face and laughed.

"Harmony!"

She let her hands fall and bit her lip. "I know. I'm sorry."

"You made it worse by laughing. You only encourage your cousin when you do that. She likes to show off for you."

"It was funny. I couldn't help myself."

"That's why we must do something now. I can't have you laughing like a lunatic at your reception."

Harmony sobered and sighed. "She doesn't like him you know."

"It's quite obvious how Bianca feels about Broderick that's why—"

Harmony shook her head. "No, I mean she doesn't like Claude."

"She's not the one marrying him."

"I know."

"And you can't listen to everything she says. Take it with a pinch of pepper."

"You mean salt," Harmony corrected.

Esther waved her hand with impatience. "Pepper, salt, it doesn't matter."

"But she thinks—"

"Who cares what she thinks? What's in your heart is all that should concern you. You've been in her shadow too long, feeling sorry for her because she lost her parents."

"I don't feel sorry for her, I admire her."

"Admiration has its place." Esther pointed to the ground. "But not here. Your heart is with Claude and his heart is with you and you are making us proud. What more is there?"

"But Bianca said—"

"Bianca says a lot of things. She's also unmarried and likely will remain so."

"Does that mean I'm not allowed to have opinions?" Bianca said.

The two women jumped and turned to find Bianca standing in the entryway of the sitting room.

"Don't get angry at the maid," Bianca said with a careless wave of her hand as she walked into the room. "I told her not to announce me." She sat down beside her cousin and said, "I love that outfit on you," admiring her cousin's fashionable green and yellow top and red skirt," before she reached and took a bite of a teacake. "Hmm…I love these."

"What do you want?" Esther said in a tight voice.

"Some company." Bianca quickly finished the teacake and wiped her hands. "It's been a dreadful morning so far."

"What happened?" Harmony said with concern.

"We don't care," Esther interrupted when Bianca opened her mouth. "We were having a private discussion."

"Yes, about me," Bianca said, taking another teacake. "What's new?"

"It means you don't always know what's best for others. You shouldn't be scaring a young girl on her wedding day."

"It isn't her wedding day yet."

Esther bristled with indignation. "Her father and I have spent—"

"Shh…" Bianca said, pressing a finger against her lips. "Wait a moment…" Bianca cocked her head and cupped her ear. "Did you hear that? What was that sound?" She paused then clapped her hands together. "Oh I know. You just made another hundred million naira."

Harmony shook her head. "You know better than to tease Mum right now, she's very stressed."

"About what?"

"About you," Esther snapped. "You reckless, jealous girl."

Bianca shook her head. "I may be reckless at times, but I'm not jealous. Just a little worried." She took her cousin's hand. "You know you can always change your mind."

Esther reached across the table and slapped Bianca's hand away then positioned herself between them. "If you listen to her, I am no longer your mother."

"Don't worry," Harmony said. "I love him."

"I'm just joking, Aunty," Bianca said, but behind her aunt she shook her head and mouthed 'No I'm not.'

Esther turned and glared at her, shifting over enough to force Bianca to move. "I can't understand why you'd take such a perfect match so lightly."

"I wouldn't say it's exactly perfect. He's a bit…simple."

"Not everyone is an intellectual Olympian," Esther shot back, shifting in her seat to force Bianca to move some more, as if trying to create as much distant between her and Harmony as she could. "He's successful, good looking and kind. He comes from a good family and will make a good husband."

Bianca shrugged with little interest. Claude was a Canadian born Nigerian with three brothers all in the sciences. Although his family's wealth didn't match Harmony's, Papa Bola's word of recommendation had held the most clout. "That's to be expected. I won't add it as a mark in his favor."

Harmony looked at her with wide eyes, casting a nervous glance at her mother. "Is it because of Broderick?"

Before her aunt could shove her off the couch, Bianca finally took her aunt's hint and stood. She sat in the chair across from them and sighed. "Why won't you put things into context? Is *what* because of Broderick?"

"The reason you don't like Claude."

Bianca thought for a moment. "You're right. I'm not impressed by his selection of friends, although like any parasite I could imagine Broderick would be hard to get rid of, but no, that's not it. I don't know what it is really. Aunty is right, ignore me. Maybe I am jealous."

Esther threw up her hands in triumph. "You see?"

"And maybe I'm right. There's just something about him that I can't put my finger on."

Her aunt shot her a look. "He's perfect."

"Is there anything about my upcoming wedding you like?" Harmony asked a little sad.

Bianca blinked surprised. "Why would you ask that?"

"You don't like the groom or his friend."

She smiled. "Don't take my words to heart. I'm just thinking aloud. Don't worry. I'll behave myself as best I can."

Harmony glanced at her mother then back at Bianca and said in an urgent voice, "Can't you try to be a little more civil with Broderick?"

"I *am* being civil," Bianca said with a sniff. "I'm resisting my natural urge to wrap my hands around his neck."

"Why do you dislike him so much?"

She laughed. "What is there to like? Dislike seems the most natural feeling when you meet a self-centered, arrogant bore like him. He's so vain he'd search for his reflection in a raindrop."

"He is handsome."

Bianca nodded. "Yes, and in case you don't notice, he'll tell you himself."

"Try…"

"I will, I promise." She affectionately blew her cousin a kiss. "Don't look so worried. All that matters is how you feel."

"I want to spend the rest of my life with Claude."

"Then that is what matters." Her watch beeped. "Oh, I'd better dash."

"Don't forget the spa appointment I made for all of us," Esther said.

"Yes, I got the timeline schedule you sent." She looked at her bare nails. "I look forward to my mani-pedi."

"You're what?"

"Manicure and pedicure." She smiled at her aunt. "I suggest you also get a massage. It helps with stress." She turned to her cousin before Esther could reply. "Don't worry, Harmony, I won't ruin your special day." She rested a hand over her heart as if making a vow. "You can trust me. I only want your happiness. Bye."

Esther waited for her niece to leave before she turned to her daughter and said, "Do you trust her?"

Harmony sighed. She wanted too, but wasn't completely sure.

Her mother pounced on her hesitation. "You do as I tell you and your wedding will be safe. Okay?"

"Okay, Mum, I'll help you," Harmony said with some reluctance."

Chapter Seven

"I didn't expect to find you here alone," Claude said, taking the empty chair at Broderick's table where he sat on the outside terrace of the hotel restaurant. A light breeze ruffled the hem of the white tablecloth and palm trees in the distance.

"I wasn't alone a few minutes ago," Broderick said with a smile. "Margaret was just here."

"I'm surprised you found the time. I only just saw you with three ladies in the hotel lounge."

"I know how to prioritize. Besides, they are leaving today anyway." He winked. "Are you sure you're ready for settling down?"

Claude's expression hardened. "Why do you do that?"

"Do what?"

"Pretend that you're a womanizer when you're not?"

"Who says I'm not?"

Claude folded his arms.

"Okay," Broderick said, letting his carefree mask slip. "It's a strategy and it's working. No woman will ever snare me in her net."

"Unless you fall in love."

"Love is a poison that drives men mad. I will abstain until my dying breath." He paused. "Although when I first saw Harmony I could see why a man could be persuaded."

Claude's gaze sharpened. "When did you first meet Harmony?"

"It was a while back. I think it was at Papa Bola's birthday party."

"Where was I?"

"I don't know," Broderick said, surprised by his friend's intense tone. "It wasn't a long conversation. I was just talking to her and liked her, but then I met her c—" He frowned at the look on Claude's face. "If I wanted your woman," he said in a low voice, pinning Claude with a dark stare, "we wouldn't be having this conversation because she'd already be mine."

Claude held Broderick's gaze for a long moment but soon felt himself unmatched by his friend's power and let his gaze fall and sighed. Broderick was not a man he would like as his enemy. "I'm sorry. I didn't mean to accuse you of anything. It's just…she's so amazing and the way the other guys look at her sometimes gets to me."

Broderick sat back as if surprised by his friend's insecurity. "She's pledged her heart to you. Announced to the world that you'll be her one and only. She's a beautiful, virgin bride from a rich family. What more can you want?"

"I know," Claude said with feeling. "It feels a little like a dream. I never thought I'd meet a woman like her."

"Well you have, so don't ruin it."

Claude fell silent for a moment then said, "I heard you were with Bianca this morning."

Broderick waved his fork. "Please. The very mention of that woman's name gives me heartburn." He glanced up and smiled when he saw Margaret approaching. "While other things make me happy."

Margaret stopped at their table. "Oh, I almost forgot to ask. Would you like to go swimming later?"

He leaned forward, resting his arms on the table. "Give me an hour."

"Okay."

"And wear as little as possible."

"Possible or legal?"

He winked. "Don't worry about legal, I know how to bribe."

She giggled. "You are a bad boy."

"Just wait 'til I'm wet."

"I can't wait." She waved then left.

Claude shook his head. "I'd be careful with that one."

"Why?" Broderick asked, watching her leave. "I plan to be anything but careful. She's fun."

"She has her snare out."

He looked at his friend. "I told you. I'm not going to get caught."

"Her mother is Harmony's aunt, so tread carefully. Family means a lot so don't ruin this for me."

"How could I do that? We're here for only a couple of days, how much trouble could I get into?"

"With Margaret, who knows? If you wanted to spend time with someone, Bianca's a choice."

Broderick let his utensils drop to his plate with a clatter. "I told you not to mention her name. It was bad enough seeing her this morning, she's not going to ruin my afternoon as well."

"Why do you let her get to you?"

Broderick sat back annoyed. He didn't know, but he'd disliked her ever since their first meeting three years ago in Italy.

He remembered telling Papa Bola and another guest about one of his adventures when she'd come into the room and interrupted him, by walking right in front of him and standing in front of Papa Bola to ask him a question.

"Didn't your mother teach you that it's rude to interrupt?" he'd said to her.

She turned to him with an expression of such feigned embarrassment it was almost comical. "I'm sorry, were you *still* talking? I thought by now you would have stopped to take a breath. If not for your sake, at least for the sake of your audience." She dipped her head with the same poignancy of a crude gesture. "I apologize." She spun away, her dark braided hair swinging against her proud shoulders, her pert nose in the air, leaving him feeling humiliated and speechless. He was never speechless, but after her rude interruption and comment he'd lost the power of his tongue.

What was worse, he was unable to recover himself because he'd also lost track of the story he'd been telling them of his trip to Gambia and briefly staying in a remote village under siege. But she made him sound petty, self-centered and uncaring. He wasn't.

Was it his fault that people liked to hear about his travels and that he enjoyed telling them? She was an irritant. One of the few—only?—women who didn't think him dashing. A woman who walked past him as if he were nothing more than something she could scrape off her shoe.

He'd taken pleasure in her predicament this morning. He'd only wished to have it last longer. It was always fun to see the stone princess knocked off her pedestal. She had nice legs, he'd noticed them more than once. Too bad their owner was atrocious, but he couldn't deny their appeal. They were dark, curvy and smooth. And the pink panties had intrigued him more than he would have liked.

But the rest of her was pure poison. He'd felt the same way when he'd first met her. She could have been dangerous to him, he was almost ready to let her snare him in her net when Papa Bola had introduced them, but then she'd flashed her teeth and bared her claws before he'd had a chance to be enchanted. It had been a lucky escape.

Unfortunately, at the wedding she would be the maid of honor (although there was nothing maidenly about her) and he the best man so her snapping brown eyes would be silently shooting insults he gladly wished to return.

"She's not that bad," Claude said.

Broderick blinked, awaking from his thoughts. "Not that bad? A woman who could make milk curdle with just a glance? A woman who could make a flower wither just by inhaling its scent? Not that bad?"

"Forget I said anything."

"I will and I warn you. Don't mention her name to me again."

Claude stood. "I'm sorry."

"Good, now let me finish my meal in peace. I have a date I'm looking forward to."

Claude nodded, but made sure Broderick didn't see the signal he'd given Papa Bola and Leonard. The plan was set.

Chapter Eight

Broderick set his utensils down and pushed his plate away. He couldn't finish his meal. The mention of Bianca always ruined his appetite. Fortunately he had something to look forward to: Margaret. He alerted the waiter and paid his tab then walked inside towards a booth were Papa Bola, Claude and Leonard sat. Since a large plant stood beside the booth, they didn't see him, so he was about to wave in greeting when he heard words that stopped him in his tracks.

"Bianca loves Broderick?" Papa Bola said in a tone of amazement. "Are you sure?"

Broderick ducked into the empty booth behind them, stunned and eager to hear more. He twisted his body to make sure his good ear didn't miss a word.

"Yes," Leonard said. "My dear Harmony told me herself. She said that Bianca's beside herself. She's unsure how she'll be able to cope at the wedding. Seeing him is painful for her."

"But she's always been so cold to him."

Broderick nodded in agreement.

"Are you sure Harmony is right?"

"Harmony told me that Bianca acts cold to protect herself," Claude said.

"Yes," Leonard said. "She's been hurt in the past and we all know that loving Broderick is not the wisest choice for a tenderhearted woman like her. She has to pretend to be hard." He paused. "I have wondered if…"

Broderick leaned in closer when Leonard stopped. *If what???*

"…if maybe I should tell him."

"No," Papa Bola said quickly. "He would only laugh. You know how Broderick is. Everything is a game to him. He likes his bachelorhood and carefree life. No one can tell him. No one must let him know her feelings. It would only hurt her more."

"True," Claude said. "I just spoke to him and he had nothing nice to say about her."

Leonard sighed. "A shame. She is a beautiful, kind woman. It is a pity that she should waste her heart on a man like him. But perhaps if he knew there was another side to her…"

Broderick nodded in agreement.

"There's no use," Claude said. "He prefers the company of Margaret."

Broderick silently swore and briefly closed his eyes.

"There's your answer," Papa Bola said. "None of us can let him find out the truth."

Leonard sighed. "Agreed. We must keep her feelings a secret."

The men got up and left the table without seeing him.

Broderick sat paralyzed. What had he just heard? Could it be true? Could Bianca really love him? Mr. Layeni had said so and Claude said that Harmony had confirmed it. Both men couldn't be wrong and Harmony was not a woman who would lie. And they all seemed to feel sorry for Bianca.

Bianca loved him? Him? A man she treated with such disdain? But they'd given him a reason for this behavior. She'd hidden her true feelings because she'd been hurt in the past. He could understand that. He'd been hurt before too.

She *loved* him.

She loved *him*.

What an astonishing revelation! Clearly she'd felt that spark of awareness when they'd first met too. It hadn't been an unrequited feeling. It had been real. And she'd fooled him into not seeing the depth of her attraction.

He had to do something. But what?

Moments later, Broderick lay on his bed and stared up at the ceiling bathed in the thought of Bianca loving him. He'd stopped by the concierge and arranged flowers be delivered to her room. He couldn't go wrong with flowers, right? Women liked flowers and she'd had an embarrassing morning. There was no harm in helping her feel a little better. That was just being considerate. Being considerate of her feelings was important.

Now he saw their meeting in the courtyard in a whole new light. No wonder she was always so snappish and wanted him far away from her. It was because she was suffering. And he'd flirted with another woman right in front of her. He regretted that now. She'd suffered all these years in silence. That would end. He wouldn't cause her anymore pain.

Loving him wasn't a mistake. He'd prove them all wrong. He never thought he'd settle with one woman, at least not yet, but he now felt a strange new urgency. He wanted to keep her love. Her heart would not be wasted on him. When he'd said he'd die a bachelor he'd never thought he'd live long enough to get married. Love wasn't a net or a poison. It was a doorway, a remedy.

His past achievements and brief affairs now felt empty and shallow. Now he had a chance to seize something that wouldn't fade.

He sat up when someone knocked on his door. "Who is it?"

"Your worst nightmare."

Bianca! "One minute," he said, jumping off the bed. He straightened his shirt and checked his reflection in the mirror before he opened the door with a smile. "What can I do for you?"

"You can stop smiling for one thing."

He glanced down at the bouquet of yellow and white roses in her hand. He'd never before noticed the dark polish of her chocolate skin, how the strands of her hair had light brown highlights under the right lighting. The scent of the roses drew him closer. "Did you need something?"

"Are both your phones off?" she said. "I tried to reach you by your hotel line and your cell phone so that you can get these." She pointed to the flowers.

Broderick pulled out his cell phone and saw the missed messages. He hadn't even heard his hotel phone ring, let alone his mobile. He'd been in such a daze. "I'm sorry, I've been…preoccupied."

"Obviously, because you—"

"I'm sorry. I didn't mean to put you through any trouble by having you coming to get me."

"If it had really been any trouble, I wouldn't be here."

"I'm thankful all the same."

"Personally, I was hoping I couldn't reach you because you'd decided to fly back home."

He nodded. "Yes, I can understand you not wanting me around."

Bianca opened her mouth, closed it then frowned. She shook her head confused. "No, you're not supposed to be understanding. You're supposed to come back with an insult."

He shrugged. "I didn't want to."

She hesitated then held up the flowers. "You sent these to the wrong room."

"No, I didn't."

"In case you didn't know, I'm not sharing a room with Margaret."

"I know that. They're for you."

She blinked. "Is this some kind of joke?"

"No. I thought you'd want something to brighten up your day after what happened this morning."

"Why?"

"I just told you why."

"I don't want them." She shoved the bouquet in his chest. "I hope you kept the receipt or you can give them to one of the ladies you were with in the lounge."

"It wasn't anything serious."

"I don't care."

He cleared his throat, glanced around then said in a quiet voice, "You don't have to pretend the other women didn't bother you or that you don't want...the flowers."

"I'm not pretending."

He lifted an eyebrow. "I think you are."

She narrowed her eyes. "What is wrong with you today? Are you sick or something? Maybe you've gotten too much sun."

He lowered his voice and said with a note of compassion. "I know."

She frowned. "You know what?"

He hesitated. It was too soon, he didn't want to push her. "You really don't want the flowers?"

Bianca rolled her eyes. "At last the synapses are working. No, I don't want them."

He took the bouquet. "Fine."

She looked at him with an odd expression then turned away.

"I'll get you something else," he said in a voice too low for her to hear. His gaze followed her as she walked down the hall, his heart picking up pace as she disappeared into her room.

He closed the door and leaned against it, holding the bouquet close. How could he have missed it? How could he have missed how her eyes lit up when she saw him? How her sharp tone was extra acidic with him all so that he couldn't see how she truly felt?

But he couldn't let her hide her feelings from him any longer. He'd let her know she was safe with him. He would prove he was worthy of her love.

She loved him and he would love her back fully, wholly and completely.

Now he had to figure out how to deal with Margaret.

Chapter Nine

The man was an idiot! What had gotten into him?

Bianca tried and failed to relax as she lay on her back, wrapped in seaweed. Her appointment at the spa was supposed to be the perfect place to get away from the madness: Her aunt's fears, her cousin's worries and now Broderick. Sneaky, cunning Broderick. What was he up to?

His behavior was totally out of character. He'd sent her flowers? He'd actually smiled at her? Was he suffering from heat stroke?

He was definitely up to something but she didn't know what. She'd have to be on her guard. She closed her eyes. She had to relax; she wouldn't let him get to her. She was going to salvage this awful day somehow. She'd enjoyed her mani-pedi and now she was alone in a private room. She took a deep breath, feeling the breeze through the open window, smelling the scent of jasmine.

"You must be joking," she heard Aunt Esther say outside the spa window. "Broderick can't be in love with Bianca."

Bianca's eyes flew open.

"Claude told me himself," Harmony replied. "And Papa Bola said Broderick's heart is completely lost."

"But that's impossible. Broderick is not the kind of man to settle on anyone."

"It's true. Dad even overheard them talking about it."

"Poor man. Bianca dislikes him so much."

"Maybe if we told her about his feelings then—"

"Absolutely not," Aunt Esther said. "She'll only find another reason to give him misery. Your cousin likes to be cruel."

Bianca frowned at that accusation.

"No, not cruel Mum," Harmony said in her defense.

Bianca nodded.

"Just a little insensitive."

Bianca frowned again. *She wasn't insensitive.*

"My point exactly," Aunt Esther said. "Can you imagine how she would make the poor man suffer if she had this knowledge?"

"But still she—"

"Must not know. Do you remember what she said about him only a few moments ago? She made her feelings about how much she dislikes him very clear."

Harmony sighed. "Although he is accomplished and funny."

"And don't forget handsome."

"Yes, my cousin is blind to it all. It's a shame really. If she'd give him a chance—"

"But your cousin is stubborn and she won't change. We will keep this a secret and never tell her. Let the poor man keep his dignity at least."

"Fortunately, after the wedding, he will not have to…" Their voices drifted away.

Bianca broke through her seaweed wrap and touched her chest. What was this? How could this be true? Broderick loved her? He cared for her so much he told his friends?

Lusty, arrogant, Broderick loved her?

Was that why he'd offered to help her in the courtyard? Was that why he'd sent her those flowers? Was that why he'd smiled at her when she went to his room?

Bianca absently drummed her fingers. He did seem strangely happy to see her. Had he teased her in front of those other women in hopes of making her jealous?

How long and how deep were his feelings for her? For him to express his feelings must mean something. And Uncle Leonard and Papa Bola were men of their word.

He loved her? Broderick *loved* her? As she was? Flaws and all? He didn't need her to change? He didn't want to fix her? He didn't find that she was too much? He loved her even though she could be loud, opinionated and maybe…just maybe…a little insensitive? *Oh don't stop*. Her heart screamed. *Love me completely!*

Suddenly her greedy heart craved his affection, the depth of her own desire shocking her. She would not laugh at him. She wouldn't tease him. His conceited ways made sense now. Perhaps he'd been trying to impress her.

Love on, Broderick. My wonderful, marvelous Broderick. Please continue to love me. You will not love alone.

Chapter Ten

She had to think. But she still didn't quite know what to think. Bianca left the spa and paced her room trying to get her thoughts in order, but they kept swirling in her mind.

She needed to find something else to focus on. Work. She would focus on work. She had some designs she hadn't committed to paper yet. She could have used her tablet, but felt like using a pencil and sketch pad instead, not trusting herself to go more high tech. Simplicity was the key to getting her thoughts back in order. To get her heart to stop beating as if it wanted to jump out of her chest.

She grabbed her portfolio and put her sketch pad and pencils inside and went to the outdoor pool. Sketching outside always helped her make sense of things. She saw an empty lounge chair and walked towards it then stopped when she saw Broderick wearing red and black swimming trunks. He stood with his back to her, rubbing something on his arm. Before, she wouldn't have noticed the broad expanse of his back, the powerful, muscular curve of his legs. Now her eyes swallowed every angle of his body.

As if he sensed her presence he glanced behind him. His eyes widened when he saw her and he spun around, hiding something behind his back.

"Oh I'm sorry," she said. "I didn't mean to startle you."

"It seems you like sneaking up on me," he said with a nervous laugh.

"No, I…What are you hiding behind your back?"

"Nothing."

She took a step forward, unable to stop a grin. "Yes, you are."

He shook his head. "It's nothing."

She jumped behind him. He spun around so she couldn't see it.

"What is it? I won't tease you, I promise." She paused. "Okay, that's a lie. I'll only tease you a little bit."

Broderick hung his head and held out the object.

Bianca glanced down at the bottle of sunscreen. She immediately felt guilty. She'd overheard that he burned easily and remembered teasing him about it. "I can't imagine a woman who'd prefer a man who burns instead of browns," she'd told him at the London party. She regretted that catty remark now.

"No wonder you always smell like coconuts and bananas," she said softly.

He sighed then set the bottle back down. "That's me. A walking tropical fruit basket."

"I like fruit baskets," she said, hoping he could hear the sincerity in her voice. "Are you sure you're putting on enough?"

He stiffened in surprise. "What?"

Bianca set her portfolio down, grabbed the bottle and spread some on her hands. "You shouldn't forget your neck. Bend down a bit. There, that's better," she said, spreading it over his skin, which felt warm under her fingers. She had to resist letting them slide down his back. She never realized she'd enjoy touching him so much.

"Thanks."

She playfully put a streak down his nose. "Don't forget your face too."

He rubbed his nose. "I usually do."

"You shouldn't."

He glanced at his watch. "I'll remember next time."

"How do you travel to hot places even though…"

"I can end up looking like a burnt tomato?" he said with a smile.

She laughed. "Yes. But taking precautions is smart." She opened her portfolio and reached for her sketch pad.

He stopped her. "You should too."

She stared at him surprised. "I should what?"

"Put on sunscreen. Just because you're darker doesn't mean you're not at risk. Here, let me show you." He took some sunscreen and spread it slowly on her arm. "See?" he said, his voice deepening with each stroke. "It doesn't have to be much."

Bianca cleared her throat, fighting to keep her pounding pulse under control. Her skin tingled from his touch, which had felt oddly sensual. "I try to stay under the shade."

"Still it doesn't hurt," he said, smoothing some more on her other arm in long, lingering strokes.

"You go red and I go black," Bianca said with a laugh although she knew her attempt at humor wasn't funny. She inwardly cringed at how ridiculous she sounded.

Broderick shook his head. "I wouldn't say that. You're more like a rum cake and this is just the icing."

"Sounds delicious."

He held up her arm and let his heated gaze travel the length of it. "Looks delicious too."

She swallowed, suddenly wanting to jump into the pool and cool off, preferably taking him with her. "Yes, well thanks."

She clumsily picked up her portfolio but her hands were slippery from the sunscreen and it slipped from her hands, spilling some of her sketches on the ground. She scrambled to gather them before they were blown into the pool. She felt relieved that she'd gotten all of them then her stomach tightened with fear when she looked up and saw Broderick studying one of them. She usually didn't let anyone see her work in its rough state.

She held her breath. *Please don't say anything.*

"What are you trying to accomplish?"

"It's nothing," she said trying to sound nonchalant. "Just an idea and it's not going well. Sketching really isn't my thing." She held out her hand eager to tuck her sketches away from his scrutiny.

He ignored her outstretched hand, glanced at his watch again then took a seat and studied the sketch some more. He then held his hand out, palm up. "May I make a few suggestions?"

She hesitated then handed him a pencil. "Sure," she managed through tight teeth. What could he know about kitchen design sketches? She should have brought her tablet. The software she used always masked her deficiencies.

"Your dimensions are slightly off and the perspective is a little skewed," he said quickly and easily adjusting her sketch until suddenly it resembled the image that had been in her head.

She stared at the altered sketched dumbfounded. "I didn't know you could draw."

He shrugged.

She took the sketch and groaned. He was really good. He'd made her initial sketch look like it had been done by a seven year old. "I hate you."

"I know."

She widened her eyes, realizing her error. "No, I didn't mean that. I mean…You're a natural."

"No, I'm not. The structure was there, I just helped a little."

"A little? I've studied for years and I still can't get the perspective in line without help from a computer."

"You had the wrong teacher."

"No, it's because I'm hopeless." She waved a finger at him. "And don't try to flatter me."

"I wasn't going to. I want you to just follow me." He took her sketch pad, turned to a blank sheet of paper and drew a few lines. "Now do that."

She did.

"And this."

She did again.

"See."

For a moment she didn't understand the random lines he'd had her imitate until she saw what he'd helped her to draw—the woman sunbathing across from them.

"Wait," Bianca said amazed. "You're a real artist."

Broderick laughed. "You're just finding that out? My photographs didn't impress you enough?"

It was hard to miss his work, which was featured online and in print, but now, instead of being annoyed she was impressed. "No, I didn't mean…stop twisting my words around. Where did you learn to draw like this?"

Broderick shrugged again, handing her the pencil. "I drew a lot as a kid."

"That's why your photographs have a painter's eye. They're beautiful and touching."

His face split into a wide grin. "So you admit you like my work?"

His smile kindled new feelings of desire. She'd remembered how he'd smiled at her three years ago in Italy and how much it had impacted her. It was no less potent now. "I love…" She stopped herself before she said too much. "…your work."

His gentle gaze held her still and his deep tone made her blood race. "I'm glad."

She cleared her throat, aware of his nearness; wanting him even closer. She heard splashing in the distance, and gripped the hard pencil in her hand, her gaze dropping to his lips. His sweet lips. "Well, of course I would like your work," she said, tearing her gaze from his mouth, before it lost its way over the beautiful wide expanse of his chest. She lifted her gaze back to his eyes. Chocolate brown eyes she could have dived into. "That's why your work is so popular."

He glanced at his watch then sighed. "Sometimes popularity is the artist's curse."

"Not all things that are popular are crass and commercial. Quality doesn't always mean niche or elite. The unwashed masses can also spot a thing of beauty."

His expression stilled. "You truly understand. Not many people do. I want my work to be accessible to everyone from a professor at a university as well to the laborer on the street."

"You've done that."

"It really means a lot to hear you say that."

The pencil snapped in her hand, startling them both. "I'm all thumbs today," she said with a nervous laugh. She stood. "I'd better go. I've taken up enough of your time and you keep glancing at your watch as if you're expecting someone."

He rose to his feet as well. "Only Margaret," he said looking suddenly uneasy. "It's just for fun, she's not really my type so you don't have to be jeal—I mean you don't have to think that there's... I just flirted with her but—"

"It's okay, a man doesn't have to explain flirting with an attractive woman."

"I was bored," he corrected. He folded his arms, the motion drawing attention to the impressive shape of his muscles and wide shoulders. "It's nothing serious."

"She may not think so. There are many women who would find you quite a catch."

"Care to name one in particular?"

"How would I be able to do that?"

He shrugged. "By being honest."

She frowned. "I don't know what you're talking about."

He leaned towards her and lifted a sly brow. "I think you do," he said letting his voice drop, "but let's pretend that you don't. However this particular woman, whoever she may be, might need to know a few things about me."

"Like what?"

"That I'm very loyal. My feelings are unwavering and I'd never hurt her, although she may have been hurt in the past."

"She's a very lucky woman then."

"And I would be a lucky man to have such a woman."

"But you don't even know who she is."

Broderick's heated gaze captured hers, his voice soft almost seductive. "I can imagine that the woman who has the good taste of loving *me* would be first of all intelligent, talented, beautiful and fun."

"And I can imagine," Bianca said in the same soft tone, "that the man who has the good taste in loving *me* would be highly successful, witty and driven."

"Don't forget handsome."

She laughed. "How could I forget that?"

"What are you two whispering about?" Margaret said. They both jumped neither having heard her approach.

"Nothing," they said in unison.

She glanced at Bianca's sketch pad. "Oh, are you still trying to draw? Remember when you got a D in drafting and cried for a week?"

Bianca snapped her sketch pad closed. "A moment I'd prefer to forget."

"It's not something to be ashamed of," Broderick said.

Margaret playfully kissed his cheek. "I've never gotten a D in my life."

Bianca took a step back. "I'll leave you two—"

"No," Broderick said in a voice that startled them both. "You could join us?"

Bianca frowned. "I'd rather not. Anyway, I didn't come to swim. Enjoy yourselves." She turned.

Broderick watched her go with regret.

Margaret sat down where Bianca had been. "Have I kept you waiting long?"

Yes, but I didn't really notice. "No," he said, his gaze continuing to follow Bianca. He had to resist the urge to let his body do the same.

Margaret watched her cousin disappear through the doors then looked at him. "She's really not your type."

He turned sharply to her. "What do you mean?"

"Just that everyone knows how much you despise her. Remember when you told me that you'd prefer the smell of sulfur over the scent of her perfume?"

He sat down. "That was a long time ago."

She laughed. "That was only this morning."

"I'm not the same man I was then."

She rested her hand on his thigh. "That's a shame because that man was a lot more fun."

Broderick removed her hand and stood. "Speaking of fun, let's go for a swim."

Margaret unlatched her robe. "Are you even curious about my swimsuit?"

But he didn't hear her when he turned and jumped into the water.

Chapter Eleven

Ursula stared at Margaret astonished. She'd been surprised when her daughter returned to their hotel room sooner than she'd expected, but what Margaret had just told her left her stunned and mortified. "You think he's *what?*"

Margaret flopped into a chair in defeat. She'd changed out of her swimsuit and now wore a simple green and yellow skirt and red blouse, a color mixture that Ursula detested since they reminded her of the colors of the flags of the two men who'd disappointed her. A musician from Benin and another from Ghana who'd decided to marry his boss's daughter instead of her, leaving her to marry a shiftless man with a weak heart who'd left her a widow at thirty years old. "I think Broderick's in love with Bianca," Margaret said.

"That's impossible. What do you mean?"

"I wouldn't believe it either, if I hadn't seen it for myself. Broderick's changed. This morning I was certain I had a chance with him." She held out her hand. "I had him in the palm of my hand. A ring and wedding bells were so close I could hear them, but this afternoon he was completely different." She gripped her hand into a fist. "And when I teased him about Bianca, he was cold to me. He was never that way before."

"B-but I don't understand. What happened?"

"I just told you," Margaret said, sliding her foot out of her high heels and wiggling her pinched toes. "He thinks he's in love with Bianca." Margaret shrugged. "It isn't entirely his fault."

"What are you talking about?"

"It's all Aunty's doing or maybe Papa Bola. I'm not quite sure. Anyway, I heard it from Harmony when I told her how odd Broderick was behaving."

"Heard what?"

"And then I saw it with my own eyes," Margaret said rubbing her foot. "Broderick thinks he's in love with Bianca now."

"That's not possible he's supposed to be in love with you."

"He isn't. But don't worry I—"

"How is your aunt involved in this?" Ursula said in a sharp tone.

"She made Harmony go along with the scheme."

Ursula frowned, leaning forward. "Scheme? There was a scheme I didn't know about?"

Margaret briefly explained what she knew then said, "Aunty did it so that Bianca and Broderick wouldn't spoil Harmony's wedding."

"But she's spoiling our plans. Broderick was meant for you. It doesn't make any sense."

"I know," Margaret said resting a hand on her chest. "How could Broderick choose Bianca over me? It was so humiliating the way he treated me at the pool as if we were just friends."

"He shouldn't have done that," Ursula said in a low angry whisper.

"I thought about telling him about the scheme. Perhaps then he—"

Ursula's lips thinned with anger. "No, you will not do that."

"Then what should I do?"

Ursula didn't know but she would come up with something. She had to. How dare Esther ruin this opportunity for them! Her dear Margaret had been humiliated. For months they had looked forward to this wedding and she'd dreamt of accepting Broderick as a son-in-law and imagining how their union would elevate her daughter's status and her own.

Esther only thought of herself and her precious daughter. She thought her dear Harmony was the sun and the moon. As pure as snow, but what would happen if all that fell apart?

"Let's put together our own scheme," Ursula said, her mind coming alive with a need for vengeance. "Your Aunty broke your heart and now it's time for someone to break hers."

Chapter Twelve

It wasn't one of her finest moments, but Bianca couldn't help herself. She needed to know more about Broderick, and Claude was her best option. She glanced around the bar, wondering if he would show up. She'd sent him a text and he'd replied but fifteen minutes had already passed.

"Sorry, I'm late," Claude said taking a seat in front of her. "I got lost looking for the Hotel Bar. I didn't realize it wasn't a name, but a location the hotel bar."

Bianca blinked. She knew Claude wasn't the brightest, but she didn't think her request would have confused him.

"I mean, it makes sense now," he continued, "but when you said 'Let's meet at the hotel bar,' I thought 'Huh, that's a strange name for a bar,' but there was this time I—"

"I'm glad you figured it out," Bianca cut in not wanting to hear more of his explanation. He was soon going to be family, being a little dense wasn't a crime. Besides, he was a loyal son who was good at helping his family's business sell medical devices.

"I know, me too. This place is enormous."

"I hope you don't mind, but I already ordered our drinks."

"I don't mind at all," he said then took a long swallow of his fizzy orange soda. She knew he had a weakness for it.

"The reason why I asked you to meet me here—"

Claude nodded as if suddenly realizing that their meeting was important. "Yes, why? You sounded kind of urgent. Is something wrong?"

"No, I just…Why didn't you tell me Broderick could draw?"

"Didn't think you'd be interested."

He had her there. "I'm not really *interested*, just curious."

"Why all of a sudden?"

"Because…of the wedding," she said seizing on the idea. "I thought I should get to know him a little better."

Claude smiled and took a sip of his drink. "He doesn't only draw, he paints too."

"Just for fun?" Bianca asked.

"No, he'd first thought of it as a career. He studied painting at the Maryland Institute College of Art. He actually paid his way by working for an interior designer who used his work for her clients. He was that good. His parents didn't really understand him though. I think he switched to photojournalism so that he could impress them. If you think about it, it's more impressive for a man to talk about being in a warzone than in a gallery."

"He worked for an interior designer?" Bianca said amazed, remembering how he'd teased her about her career designing kitchens. But she'd read him wrong all this time. Was that what had first attracted him to her?

"Yes. He'd worked for Coliseum Inc."

She paused. The company was affiliated with a big construction company that built buildings around the DC metropolitan area.

"You've probably seen his paintings in a hotel or conference room and never even noticed," Claude said.

There were so many things she hadn't noticed about him before and now she couldn't get enough. There were so many layers to such an extraordinary man.

"Anything else you want to know?" Claude said with a grin.

"Well, now that you asked…" Bianca began then stopped when she saw Claude's expression become a storm cloud as he stared at something behind her. "What is it?" she asked, turning to see what had captured his attention.

"What is Harmony doing here?"

"That's not Harmony," Bianca said watching her cousin Margaret flirt with one of the bartenders. But Bianca could understand his mistake, with the low light, similar colored outfit her cousin Harmony had been wearing earlier that day and only her profile, Margaret and Harmony did look alike. But Harmony's manner was more reserved than Margaret's. She turned back to Claude. "You should know Harmony would never do that."

His expression softened. "You're right."

"Trust is a two-way street."

"I know." He suddenly smiled his jovial mood back in place as if nothing had happened. "What more did you want to know about Margaret…I mean Broderick?"

Bianca stood. "I think you've told me enough. Thanks."

"No problem and don't worry, I'll pay for the drinks."

"Thanks," Bianca said suddenly finding it hard to smile at him while her mind repeated the sight of his thunderous expression only moments before. She left the bar with a sinking feeling she couldn't put into words.

Chapter Thirteen

The afternoon sun touched the tips of the bouquet Broderick had sitting on his side table, while he flipped through the TV channels, briefly landing on a drama and a preacher in a three thousand dollar suit, talking about the importance of selling possessions and giving to the poor.

He had hoped a swim would have dampened his ardor, but he felt even more eager to be with Bianca. Margaret had been fun—Margaret was always fun—but after his conversation with Bianca he hadn't realized how much he wanted more substance. How much the sound of her voice was like music.

And she liked his work, understood his passion. Understood him and loved him. Cared about him. He briefly closed his eyes remembering the feel of her soft fingers on his skin as she rubbed sunscreen on the back of his neck. He'd never known that such a simple act could feel so erotic.

He'd be patient with her. He'd been reckless before, blind to how she'd felt about him, but now that he knew how she felt he'd be cautious, compassionate.

If only Margaret hadn't come and ruined things. He didn't like seeing Bianca teased about having a bad mark.

But that wasn't it. He hated her reminding him of how cruel his remarks about Bianca had been in the past.

He glanced at the flowers, and reached out and touched one velvet petal with the tips of his fingers. She hadn't liked his gift. Perhaps there was something else he could get her. Jewelry maybe? No, she didn't wear a lot. Perhaps a carving? Yes, a carving could work. His former boss at Coliseum used to adore them. She and her husband were always traveling the globe looking for unique carvings for their clients to choose from. Maybe Bianca, being a designer too, would like the same.

But finding the right carving could be risky. He didn't know her house décor. He didn't want to give her anything that wouldn't match her artistic sensibilities. He pulled out his cell phone and called the one person he trusted to help him.

Minutes later Harmony sat in Broderick's hotel room, staring at him wide eyed. The text he'd sent her, asking her to come to his room, had been unexpected. He was Claude's friend and she'd never been alone with him. And being aware of his wild reputation, she'd almost declined, but curiosity had gotten the best of her and because her parents had taken charge of her wedding, she had some time to spare.

When she'd entered his room and seen the eager way he'd ushered her to a seat, at his small corner table, as if she were an honored guest he'd been waiting for, her curiosity had only grown.

He seemed younger somehow and without the biting, cutting remarks he was usually tossing at her cousin, she couldn't help but notice how handsome he was and to her embarrassment she found herself feeling a little shy when he smiled at her. But when he'd shared his plans, she'd been stunned. "You want to buy a carving for Bianca?"

"Yes, this wouldn't be one of those cheap, mass produced ones you'd find in the market for tourists. This would be done by a true artisan." He held out his cell phone to show her the screen. "I even have some samples to show you."

Harmony waved the cell phone away, not wanting to deepen her part of the deception. "I don't think you should."

"You don't think she'll like it?" He pointed to the bouquet. "I sent her flowers, but she didn't like them."

Harmony rubbed her forehead in dismay. "No, I think you shouldn't think of spending anything else on this trip."

"It won't be a problem."

"But you shouldn't."

"But I can—"

"Bianca doesn't like carvings," she lied. She knew that her cousin would love one, but didn't want Broderick spending his money needlessly. When the wedding was over, perhaps they would come to their senses when they were back in the States.

Broderick frowned. "She doesn't?"

"No."

"Does she like jewelry?"

"No, she…she doesn't like when men spend money on her. It makes her uneasy."

He nodded. "Oh, because she's been hurt."

"Yes," Harmony said quickly, glad that he'd given her a reason. "All the men who have showered her with gifts have hurt her. So it's best not to buy her anything, okay?"

"Okay." He fell quiet a moment then said, "Not even—"

"Nothing."

He nodded looking a little sad. "Okay."

Harmony hated the look of dejection on his face, but she knew it was for his own good. She left his room, pleased she'd stopped a possible disaster, unaware that someone was watching her.

Chapter Fourteen

"It's getting out of hand," Harmony said. She paced in front of her parents as they sat together on the couch.

"Why are you moving to and fro like a confused goat?" Esther said. "That's something your cousin would do. Sit down or you'll look peakish on your wedding day."

Harmony sat and took a deep breath. "But—"

"Have you contacted the photographer?" Esther asked her husband.

"Yes," Leonard replied checking his cell phone. "He knows when to arrive,"

"Mum, Dad," Harmony said. "I—"

"Take another deep breath," Esther said, looking at her own cell phone. "The makeup and gele artist hasn't gotten back to me."

"I heard from her," Leonard said. "I've received a response from all the vendors as well. Everything is ready."

Harmony made a sound of frustration. "You're not listening to me!"

Esther and Leonard looked at her stunned.

Esther put her cell phone away and looked at her daughter with concern. "Deep breaths, take—"

"I don't need deep breaths."

"It's not like you to be so agitated."

Harmony waved her hands. "Because it's getting out of control."

"What is?" Leonard asked.

"Broderick and Bianca. Claude just told me that Bianca asked him about Broderick's art skills."

"I didn't know he had any," Esther said.

"Neither did I," Harmony said. "But that's not the point. She was asking Claude questions about *Broderick*. I think she's really fallen for him."

"So?"

"And Broderick really thinks he's in love too. He came and found me to ask me what to buy her."

Esther clapped her hands and beamed. "So our plan worked." She stood up and raised her hands to the sky. "Praise be."

"Mum, he's thinking of something expensive."

She looked at her daughter unconcerned. "What's the problem with that? He's not hurting for funds."

Harmony shook her head. "That's not the point. It's deceitful."

Esther sat down beside her. "But their feelings are real. At first you were worried they would ruin your wedding..."

"I wasn't worried, *you* were."

"...But now everything is perfect," she continued.

Harmony looked at her father for support. "You know this is wrong. You should have seen Broderick's face when I told him not to buy Bianca anything."

"We've come too far to do anything about it now," he said resigned.

"There's nothing to worry about," Esther said, taking her daughter's hand. "It's just wedding jitters. You're looking for trouble when it doesn't exist. Just rest. Hours from now you'll be a beautiful bride and starting a new life. Trust us, we've done this for you. Now only think of your special day."

Harmony forced a smile, wishing she could.

Chapter Fifteen

Samuel Victor Pride Alabi, Slick for short, was a man who liked causing trouble. It wasn't the first time he'd made a dirty video in an expensive hotel, but it was the first time he'd gotten paid for it. He walked out of the bedroom buttoning his crumpled green shirt.

Ursula stood from her position on the couch. "Is it done?"

"The lighting could have been better," he said. It was something he said often and didn't mean.

"I don't need high quality," she snapped. "I want it simple and quick. You made sure her face wasn't shown?"

"Yes, mah."

"And you said her name?"

He nodded. "Yes, mah. More than once."

She handed him the envelope thick with cash. "You don't need to count it."

"No, mah," he said quickly flipping through the money and tallying the amount. "But does it include a bonus?"

"A bonus?"

He licked his finger and flipped through the money again. "Sometimes my tongue gets loose."

She handed him some more.

"Sometimes it likes to whisper."

She handed him a few more. He grinned and tucked the money away. "Thank you, mah." He glanced at Margaret who stood in the bedroom doorway. "It's been a pleasure."

A few yards away, Andrew Olawale watched Slick pocket the money then leave the fine hotel room. He knew he'd only get crumbs for the video he'd recorded. He quietly followed behind. One day he'd be able to afford a room in a hotel like this and he would no longer be invisible. One day he'd sing in front of a crowd of thousands just like his favorite singer. But right now, when he wasn't helping Slick, he made his living as a scavenger on the Olususun landfill site. As an overachiever, he didn't go at anything by halves. He told himself that if he had to scavenge why not go for the largest dump site in the city?

But he kept his job a secret. Nobody knew what he did. They all thought he made his money from his music and working with Slick and he preferred it that way.

One day he'd have a website where people could listen to his music. Lots of now internationally famous musicians had come from his ghetto, a place where the streets rocked every night to a party going on somewhere.

He wasn't ashamed, he made money and a man had to support himself and his passion and right now his passion was his music. He lived and breathed it. He sang every day, and every night a new song came to him itching to be born. What these rich people threw away didn't make sense, so many things that were perfectly good; he'd given a teddy to his niece and one time he'd found a camera with loads of memory. They'd toss away a fresh breeze if they could.

Soon a song sprang up in his mind of what he'd just witnessed. Of the crazy things rich people do. Of deception. He hadn't been paid to keep quiet and the song told a tale of deception that many would find hard to believe…

Chapter Sixteen

*"T*he moon has become a dancer at this festival of love..."*

Bianca stopped outside of Broderick's hotel room. She had just returned from dinner in her aunt and uncle's suite, her aunty smiling at her in a way she'd never seen before. Clearly the closer the wedding day came, the brighter her mood. However, Bianca's mood still hadn't lifted since her conversation with Claude, but she didn't know what to do about it.

Those thoughts had been occupying her mind as she walked down the empty hall to her room when she heard Broderick's voice. She walked closer to the door he'd left ajar and listened as if his words had wrapped themselves around her like a spell.

"...This divine love, beckons us, to a world beyond, only lovers can see, with their eyes of fiery passion."

And as he continued the poem of a divine love, of chosen lovers and their fiery passion, that same passion filled her. That's when she saw them together, their souls and bodies intertwined. Especially their bodies.

She leaned against the door weak with longing, but too late remembered that it was partially opened and fell with a thud into the room. Her image of them bursting like a bubble.

Broderick rushed to her side. "Are you okay?"

She jumped to her feet, her cheeks burning from embarrassment. "I'm sorry. Your door was open and I couldn't help listening. I didn't mean to interrupt."

Broderick motioned to a chair. "You didn't."

Bianca hesitated then took the offered seat. "What poem was that?"

He closed the door then lifted the large book of poems he'd left open on the table. "*The Privileged Lovers* by Rumi," he said. "It's for the reception. Claude wanted me to say a few words. What do you think?"

Read to me some more. All. Night. Long. "I-I think it's beautiful. You can't miss."

He closed the book then tapped the cover with his forefinger, studying her face. "Hmm."

Bianca looked around his room, feeling suddenly uneasy by his gaze and his silence. Silence was not something that usually happened between them. There wasn't much to see. His room was similar to hers with the dark wood bed frame, cream colored sheets and purple decorative pillows then her gaze fell on the flowers. "You kept them."

Broderick turned and looked at the bouquet with a rueful smile. "Yes."

"Would you paint that?"

He turned sharply to her. "Who told you I paint?"

She flashed a coy smile. "I have my sources."

He sat down. "I don't do it anymore."

"Why not?"

"Busy. But…" He leaned forward, his voice deepening. "I could be persuaded to start again."

A shiver of delight coursed through her. "How?"

"If I found the right model."

She's right here waiting. Bianca tugged on the collar of her blouse, feeling warm. "I'm sure that wouldn't be difficult."

"It's more difficult than you think." He stood and came around the table. "You see I can be very particular," he said lifting her chin, then letting his gaze measure the rest of her. "First I must find her beautiful." His finger gently traced the line of her jaw and her cheekbone, his burning gaze holding her still. "Someone that I'd never tire of looking at."

"And if you found her?" Bianca said in a breathless whisper, an aching hunger building within her.

Broderick pulled her to her feet then swept her into his arms. "I'd want her completely naked." He set her down on the bed.

Bianca stared up at him. "Completely?"

He nodded. "Completely."

She took off her blouse. "Like this."

He lifted an eyebrow. "That's a start."

Bianca began to unlatch her bra then stopped. "And what will you be doing?"

Broderick rested his hands on his hips, his roving gaze stripping her bare. "Enjoying the view."

Bianca covered her chest, feeling suddenly exposed and vulnerable. "But there are no paints or easel or even a tablet for you to use."

He shrugged. "So?"

"I can't get naked for no reason."

Broderick took off his shirt. "Then I'll give you one," he said before he covered her mouth with his.

Chapter Seventeen

That night Bianca discovered that ecstasy had a flavor—tropical fruit with a hint of spice. It had a texture too—tight black curls, taut brown nipples and smooth skin that seemed designed to be touched and tasted.

She surrendered to the hard body on top of hers as hands she'd once despised searched and discovered her pleasure points. Had she really once hated this man? Had she really once hated a man who she now eagerly welcomed inside her body and whose arousal now stirred her senses into a fevered frenzy of desire?

How could her heart have been so blind to what her body knew and now craved? For she craved him and his love even more than when she'd first learned she had it. She knew she'd become greedy but couldn't help it. So much time she'd wasted that she wished to reclaim, so much damage she wanted to rebuild. She wondered who she used to be before this moment.

Broderick wondered the same thing as Bianca tightened around him, the liquid heat between her thighs coating his arousal. As he felt her hot soft flesh against his, he wondered how he could ever have thought her cold. How he could ever have had such disdain against a woman so warm and willing? A woman so perfect for him?

Only the sounds of their pleasure and hunger against the whisper of shifting sheets filled the room; the fragrance of roses scenting the air as they passed the night without words, letting their bodies say all that needed to be said.

With a light touch to his inner thigh Bianca said, "I love you."

With a kiss behind her ear he said, "I know. I love you too."

With a glance she said, "Is this really happening?"

With a smile he said, "Yes, you're not dreaming."

And with a soft sigh of satisfaction she said, "If I were dreaming, I'd never want to wake up."

And with a low groan he said, "Me too."

Broderick held her close, pressing kisses along her shoulder as she lay in his arms.

Bianca started to speak then, shifted her position and said, "Oh, I should probably be on this side so you can hear me better."

He stiffened.

"It's nothing to be ashamed of."

He closed his eyes.

"I think it's sexy."

He opened his eyes and stared at her stunned. "What?"

"Just testing to see which ear works."

He frowned. "So you don't think it's sexy?"

She kissed his ear, then said in a silky voice. "I think everything about you is sexy." She kissed his other ear then his mouth. "Everything," she said meeting his wary gaze.

Broderick held her gaze but didn't smile.

Bianca bit her lip wondering if she shouldn't have brought it up. Claude had warned her. "Forget I mentioned it. You don't have to tell me what happened. And I don't want you to remember that day." She slowly let her hand slid up his chest. "All that matters is that you survived and you're here with me."

He closed his eyes and swallowed. "I don't want to think about it."

"I know," she said softly. *I'm sorry.*

"I don't want to think about it," he repeated with pain in his voice.

"I know."

"I don't want…" He let his words fall away as tears seeped from under his lids.

Bianca hugged him close. "You're safe with me. I'm so glad you made it through."

Broderick pressed his palm against one eye. "I made some mistakes." He shook his head. "I was where I shouldn't have been. I'd gotten cocky."

"I don't care." She tried to pull his hand away.

He pressed harder. "If I hadn't—"

"I don't care. Open your eyes and look at me."

He shook his head. "Bianca," he said, her name a whisper on his lips.

"Please."

He let his hand fall then slowly did.

She cupped his face in her hands. "Think of me. Think of this. Think of nothing else. Think about how good it feels to be alive."

Broderick sat up. "I need some air." He grabbed his boxers and opened the window.

Bianca didn't move. He needed space from her; she knew the window was just an excuse. Did he think she was too much? Had she been too forceful? Was his love more fragile than she thought? Or was she so strong she could destroy anything?

Broderick hung his head and released a heavy sigh. "What is wrong with you?"

"What?"

"How long do you expect me to stand here all by myself?"

"You said you wanted some space."

He frowned. "Did I say that?"

No, he hadn't. He'd said he needed some air. She'd made up the rest on her own. *She* was the one who was fragile. The one quick to take offense. Being in love wasn't about constantly being on the defensive. It meant trusting him no matter how vulnerable that made her feel. She wrapped the sheet around her body and joined him at the window. She looked out at the jewel colored city at night, knowing other parts of the country were in darkness. She knew how lucky they were.

"I've never told anyone this," Bianca said in a quiet voice, keeping her gaze on the city lights afraid she'd lose courage if she looked at him, "but I think you're the one person who would understand. When I was in college, I liked to party. After one long late night party I drove home when I shouldn't have. I wasn't drunk, but I was tipsy and that was enough. I was a few blocks from my house; I don't even remember how I got that far, when I hit something.

"I scrambled out of the car to see what it was and discovered the victim: A cat. A sweet little ginger named Buster. He was the pride of my elderly neighbors who'd gotten him as a kitten and had owned him for seven years. He was their life. I couldn't believe what I'd done.

"I sobered up fast but it was too late. The cat died and I buried it. For nearly a year the couple posted "Lost cat" signs all over town and I lived with my guilt and my stupidity. I could have killed something else that night, something that couldn't be buried." She turned to look up at him, her face burning with shame. "So I know what being overconfident looks like and the consequences. And I also had to face my cowardice that I couldn't tell anyone what I'd done. I hated myself for that. Still do sometimes."

He nodded.

"After that I tried to be the best neighbor. I made sure they got a new kitten. Helped them with their groceries. They thought I was an angel and every time they thanked me I felt like a fraud. They died a day apart and even at their funeral their daughter said how much they loved me and how much of a comfort I'd been to them after losing Buster." Bianca lowered her head and wiped away a tear. "She told me how I'd made their final years a joy."

"But you had," Broderick said, lifting her face. "That wasn't a lie."

"But the reason why I helped them was."

"But the outcome was the same. You paid your penance. Stop punishing yourself."

She nodded. "I will if you'll stop being ashamed that you're partially deaf."

He released a heavy sigh, groaned then pulled her into his arms, holding her tight. "Easier said than done."

"I know."

He drew away and searched her eyes. "I still don't want to talk about it."

She nodded. "I know."

He bit his lip. "But when I'm ready…"

"I'll be here." She lightly brushed her lips against his then turned towards the bed. "Now I've got to go." She took off the sheet and started to change.

"Why?" Broderick said disappointed. "You can spend the night."

"No, I can't. I have to get up early tomorrow."

He snatched her blouse before she could put it on. "Why?"

She laughed and held out her hand. "Give it back."

He hugged it close and pulled a face. "Why do you have to leave?"

She smiled at his pitiful expression. "Because it's my cousin's wedding day."

"So?"

"And as the maid of honor I have a lot to do. There's getting the bride ready, hair, makeup—"

"Okay, okay. I get the picture." Broderick sat on the edge of the bed and reluctantly handed her the blouse. "I suppose as the best man I have some things to do too."

Bianca pulled on her blouse. "Yes. I'll see you tomorrow. Sweet dreams."

He walked her to the door. "Same."

"I can't stay tonight, but tomorrow night will be different."

His smile returned. "I look forward to it," Broderick said then watched her enter her room before he returned to bed. He got under the warm sheets, inhaling her scent which still lingered on them, his smile still in place. Tomorrow night he'd get to wake up with her in his arms. They'd share breakfast together and have the day to themselves.

He was halfway asleep when a terrible realization gripped him. He wouldn't get to see her tomorrow night because he'd already scheduled his return flight to leave immediately after the reception.

Chapter Eighteen

He dare not breathe.

Claude sat on his bed staring at the image on his cell phone in shock. He couldn't believe his eyes.

He'd brushed Aunt Ursula's comments aside when she'd hinted that Harmony wasn't as pure as she seemed. He even ignored the photo she'd shown him of Harmony coming out of Broderick's hotel room.

But this.

This made his blood run cold. Harmony in bed with another man.

She had made a fool out of him. She'd made him wait months for something she'd given freely. How her family must have been laughing at him. Were they trying to foist her off their hands? That had happened to a friend of his who'd married a girl who had a kid that wasn't his. He didn't find out the truth until the kid got sick and needed a transplant. And the blood test showed that the child wasn't his.

He knew it was all too good to be true. Harmony had been like a dream to him, but it had all been a lie. What other secrets was Harmony hiding? Would she spring an unexpected pregnancy on him too? Did her family think he was stupid?

Claude turned off his cell phone and gripped his hands into fists. He would prove them wrong.

Chapter Nineteen

"I know a groom's supposed to be jumpy," Broderick said as he stood beside Claude in the church waiting for the bride to arrive, "but you're taking it to another level." He couldn't understand his friend's sour mood. The day was stunning, the bright sun reminding him of the sweet tangerine he'd had for breakfast as it blazed above the white chapel.

Claude didn't look at him. He kept his steely gaze focused ahead. Broderick shrugged, attributing his friend's strange behavior to nerves. Teasing him probably wouldn't help.

He turned when the sound of the wedding march filled the church. His gaze passed over the wave of colorful geles, the green and gold *aso ebi* of the bride's family complementing the extravagant silver lace of the groom's family, and fell on Bianca who wore an off-the-shoulder, floor length gown, her hair piled high on her head while long gold earrings swung from her ears, and for a moment he imagined that she was coming to him. He had to wipe the image away so that he didn't embarrass himself and say 'I do' instead of the groom.

Harmony beamed, she was a vision of loveliness on her father's arm. Broderick glanced at Claude to see his reaction, but his steely expression was still firmly in place. Broderick frowned finding it strange that the sight of Harmony hadn't softened his friend's features even a little bit.

She smiled at Claude.

He didn't smile back.

Broderick nudged him with his elbow, wondering if his friend was so nervous that he'd forgotten how.

Moments later the bride and groom stood side by side in front of the pastor and the ceremony began.

And just as quickly ended when Claude said in a voice of controlled rage, "I can't marry a woman who lies."

For a moment nobody spoke.

Broderick nudged him again and said in a low voice. "Have you been drinking?"

"No."

"I think—"

He turned to him, his eyes dark. "I know what I said. I can't marry a woman who says one thing but does another." He turned to Harmony. "Why did you make such a fool out of me? So publicly flaunting your purity and then in darkness doing something else?"

Harmony stared at him in distress. "I don't know what you're talking about."

"I saw you. I saw the video of you with that man."

"What man?"

Broderick grabbed his arm, alarmed. "I don't think—"

Claude yanked his arm away. "Of course you'd stand up for her. I saw her come out of your hotel room."

Broderick blinked then looked at Bianca, shocked at the implication being made. "Nothing happened."

"Maybe not with you, but I saw her with someone else."

"I wasn't with anyone," Harmony said.

Claude turned to someone and gave them a signal, within seconds the lights went off and an image appeared on the far wall behind the pastor. It showed an intimate scene of a woman who looked like Harmony and a man screaming her name.

The crowd gasped.

"Turn it off!" the pastor demanded. "I will not have these sacred walls stained with such filth!"

The video stopped and the lights returned.

"What are you doing?" Harmony asked Claude, hurt and confused.

"Showing the world who you really are," he said in a cold voice.

Leonard stood. "Someone has deceived you."

"The deception is yours," Papa Bola countered rising to his feet. "You've tried to deceive us all. I heard from a reliable source about the behavior of this woman."

"What source?" Esther said, surging to her feet.

Ursula slowly rose to her feet, her eyes cast down in regret. "I'm sorry sister, but I could not pretend not to see what I did," she said lifting her gaze.

Esther collapsed into her seat as if she'd been struck.

Papa Bola looked at Broderick. "Do you deny she was in your room?"

Broderick held out his hands in amazement. "I told you nothing happened. I called her—"

"What woman of purity would go to a man's room alone at such an hour?"

"It wasn't that late," Broderick said with a laugh. "I only—"

"A man known for his way with women," Papa Bola continued. "Don't worry. I do not blame you."

"But we didn't do anything. This is ridiculous. If you will just let me explain—"

"And aside from that untoward behavior, the video we've all now witnessed is proof of her true nature." Papa Bola pressed his hand over his heart. "I am ashamed that I recommended my dear friend to such a shameless woman."

Harmony gasped in pain and dismay then ran out of the church.

Chapter Twenty

Ursula laughed until her sides ached. The look on Esther's face had been priceless. And Leonard's! She laughed harder. From across their hotel room Margaret stared at her with a frown.

"Mum—"

"Wasn't that wonderful? It was better than I could have predicted." She wiped away tears.

"I don't think it was fair to get Broderick in trouble too."

She shrugged. "He's a grown man who can handle himself."

"But only Claude was supposed to see the video. What if…"

"There is nothing to worry about."

"The entire church—"

"Saw what we wanted them to see."

Margaret sat beside her mother and rubbed her hands together anxious. "What if someone finds out?"

"Nobody will," Ursula said with a dismissive wave of her hand. "It's all over now. The wedding is ruined." She clicked her tongue with false pity. "All that money gone to waste," she said then amusement left her eyes, replaced with a look of deep seated envy that still burned within her. "Serves them right."

Chapter Twenty-one

The hotel suite held the heaviness of a wake.

Harmony stayed locked up in her parent's bedroom, Esther wept on the couch, Leonard stood staring sightlessly outside the window and Bianca paced.

"How will we recover from this shame?" Leonard asked no one in particular.

"The shame is not ours," Bianca snapped. "It's Papa Bola's and Claude's. She is innocent, Uncle. Shame on them for spreading vicious lies."

He spun around to her. "Claude and Papa Bola are not storytellers. There must have been some truth to their suspicions. Even your aunt saw her coming from Broderick's room."

"He said nothing happened and I believe him."

"Only because you've become blinded by a love that isn't real."

"What do you mean?"

He shook his head. "Never mind."

Bianca hesitated, wanting to pursue the strange statement, but she pushed the idea aside instead. Her uncle was upset and didn't know what he was saying. "Even if I didn't believe Broderick, I believe Harmony. And I know her actions were innocent. I've been to a man's—"

"She is not you. She should know better."

"So should you!"

Leonard's gaze sharpened, but his voice grew soft. "You dare raise your voice at me?"

Bianca bit her lip.

The room fell silent aside from the sound of Esther's cries.

Bianca took a deep, steadying breath. "Uncle, I say this with the utmost respect to you, please don't be blinded by Papa Bola's status and the admiration you have for him. Instead listen to your heart and trust in the child you raised. We both know Harmony and we know she could never have done what they said."

Leonard lowered his head but didn't respond.

Bianca stormed out of the suite. How could her aunt and uncle believe such lies! Her cousin had endured a verbal massacre and she hadn't been able to protect her. She'd sensed something was wrong with Claude, but the truth had revealed itself too late. He had a terrible jealous streak.

Bianca stumbled into the hallway and leaned against the wall, her legs no longer able to hold her. She slid to the ground and cried.

She quickly wiped her eyes when she heard the elevator doors open and footsteps come down the hall. She shot to her feet.

"Bianca?"

She didn't turn at the sound of Broderick's voice, instead she walked towards her room.

"How is she?"

Bianca halted and spun around. "She might as well be dead. And my uncle soon will make her dead to him."

Broderick took a step towards her, his voice gentle. "You've been crying."

She nodded unashamed. "And I will cry until my soul is empty."

"I don't like to see you cry."

"Then leave me alone because I have more tears to shed."

He took her arm. "No, come on. Let me take you to your room."

Moments later they sat together on the edge of her bed.

Broderick shook his head in anger and confusion. "I think there's been a mistake. I don't know how or why, but something's wrong. It's not like Claude to blow something so innocent out of proportion. He used to trust me."

Bianca looked at him with hope, sensing an ally. "So you don't believe the video?"

He sniffed. "Of course not."

"I would give my life to any man who could prove my cousin's innocence."

Broderick folded his arms. "You don't have to give me your life because I'll do whatever you need me to." He took her hand in his, his voice deepening with emotion. "I know this might sound crazy, but I love you more than I've ever loved anyone before."

For a few seconds Bianca didn't speak, keeping her gaze fixed on their hands, but when she finally did, her voice held the weight of her heart. "You're not the only crazy one." She swallowed, took a deep breath then met his gaze. "Because until this moment, I didn't know that a broken heart could still love. But I know it does because I love you too. More than I've loved anyone."

He squeezed her hand then kissed the back of it. "Tell me what you want me to do."

"I want you to find Claude."

He nodded. "And?" he pressed when she stopped.

"And I want you to put a bullet through his heart."

Broderick released her hand and laughed. "You must be joking. Never in a million years."

Bianca shot to her feet, her eyes blazing. "He spread such vile allegations. He slandered her name in front of her family and friends. On the very soil where she was born, in the very church where she was baptized. He opened his mouth and spread such filth without mercy. Why should a man like that still breathe?" She tapped her chest. "If I were a man—"

"Bianca."

"Or if I knew a man who would avenge Harmony for my sake I would applaud him. She deserves revenge because she has been viciously treated. While all you brave and honorable men do nothing. Papa Bola siding with him, her own father doubting the child he'd carried in his arms as a baby and you…thinking of your friendship more than your friend's cruelty."

He stood, helpless. "Bianca, I love you, but—"

"Your love is just words. A woman could starve on such a diet."

"Do you want me to prove it?"

She shook her head, weary. "Go, I have to help my cousin on my own."

"Do you have no doubt that your cousin is innocent?"

She shot him a look. "Do you?"

Broderick rested his hands on his hips and sighed resigned. "Then she must be avenged. Go comfort your cousin." He turned to the door.

"Where are you going?"

"I'm going to do as you asked," he said in a voice edged with steel, "and make Claude pay."

Chapter Twenty-two

He couldn't find Claude, the coward. His family would certainly be no help.

Broderick sat in his hotel room trying to strategize his next step, but falling short. He couldn't get a hold of Papa Bola either. He wouldn't be surprised if he had helped in Claude's disappearance.

He straightened when he heard a knock on the door. He answered and saw the hotel maid Miss Lovely. "May I clean your room, sah?"

He opened the door wider and stepped back. "Yes, come in."

Broderick returned to his chair and closed his eyes. He would have to change his flight and spend a few more days if he wanted to get to the bottom of things.

If only he knew exactly what was going on. He heard the turn of the faucet as water rushed in the bathtub and Miss Lovely's voice echoed in the room as she sang.

"You all think it's me.

But just you wait and see.

Your eyes will tell you lies.

But that is fine with me.

Because I want to see you hurt.

Because I want to see you cry.

So believe what you see.

Because I want to see you die."

Broderick opened his eyes. Something about her lyrics felt familiar. Too familiar.

He walked into the bathroom and saw her scrubbing the tub. "What was that?"

She jumped to her feet, alarmed. "Oh, sorry, sah. Was I too loud?"

"No," he said quickly, not wanting her to be frightened. "You know I enjoy your singing. I just wondered about your song."

She flashed a wide smile. "My brother, Andrew, wrote it last night in a white heat. He sometimes makes up songs from real life. He said this song wouldn't leave him. It took him only fifteen minutes to write it and he sang it to me. And now I can't stop singing it too."

"It sounds like a story."

"It is, about a woman pretending to be someone else to make her man jealous."

Everything clicked as things he hadn't noticed before came into sharp focus. Why Margaret had looked more guilty than shocked when he'd seen her face in the church. Why he'd caught Aunt Ursula sending a look at Aunt Esther.

Broderick grabbed Miss Lovely by the shoulders and kissed her on the cheek. "Thank you, you are an angel." He pulled out his wallet. "Does your brother know any more songs?"

Chapter Twenty-three

It had taken a lot of pleading, but Harmony finally let Bianca into the bedroom with her. Bianca had expected to find her cousin hidden under the covers and pillows, her eyes swollen from crying, but instead she found Harmony changed out of her wedding dress, wearing faded jeans and a light yellow T-shirt, her eyes were red, but her expression was calm.

"I wish I had listened to you," Harmony said. She sat on the bed and folded her legs. "You were right about everything."

Bianca sat in front of her. "This is not the time for 'I told you sos'. Broderick will take care of Claude for you." She nodded with cruel pleasure when her cousin's eyes widened. "Yes, I told him to avenge your—" She stopped when Harmony slapped her across the face. Bianca touched her stinging cheek and stared at her stunned. "What was that for?"

"For your stupidity."

Bianca's brows shot up. "My stupidity? I-I understand you're upset," she said stumbling over her words, "but don't take your anger out on me."

"I'm not. I'm angry at you for my own reasons."

"What did I do wrong?"

"Isn't there enough misery? Why would you ask Broderick to do such a thing?"

"Isn't it obvious? Because—"

"Because what? Because you want him to prove himself to you? Are you proud of how well you can use him?"

"I just thought—"

"I can fight my own battles. I'm not as weak as people think. I thought you would know that."

Bianca stared at her speechless.

"Did you even once consider how he must feel?" Harmony continued. "Claude is his friend."

"Why are you talking to me this way?" Bianca said wounded by her cousin's scolding. "I did it for you."

"Did I ask you to?"

"No, but Claude should pay—"

"I know," Harmony said softening her tone. "But not like this. Not using a man's feelings for you as a weapon." She gripped her hands into fists and closed her eyes. "I'm tired of all these lies and manipulations. I'm sick of how we use each other."

What lies and manipulations? "I wasn't using him."

Harmony stared at her. "Do you believe that he loves you?"

Bianca hesitated. *I heard you say it.* "I don't know."

"Do you love him?"

Yes. "I don't know that either."

Harmony's eyes filled with tears, when she spoke, her voice was barely a whisper. "Don't lie to a woman whose heart is broken."

Bianca lowered her gaze, feeling her cousin's pain. "It happened so suddenly, it's hard for me to say it aloud." She lifted her eyes. "But, yes, I do love him."

"And he'll do anything for you and you wasted that love on your hatred for Claude."

"But—"

Harmony looked sad and covered Bianca's hand with hers. "Don't you see how close you came to treating him as Claude treated me?"

Fear gripped her heart, her cousin's words stinging as her slap had. "That's not true."

"Today I learned a valuable lesson. I watched the man I loved believe lies about me and take his love away. And that's when I knew that any love that can quickly change, that can easily be withheld for any reason, is not true love at all."

Chapter Twenty-four

With cunning, bribery and threats, Broderick was able to track down Claude, Papa Bola and get them and Ursula and Margaret to join him in the Layeni's suite to tell them all what he'd uncovered.

Claude stared at Broderick as if he was about to be sick. "It's not her?"

"No."

"But—"

"Did you think to authenticate what you saw before making allegations?"

"How was I supposed to do that? It came to my phone the night before my wedding. I consulted with Papa Bola and he was also stunned. We had proof."

"What proof?" Broderick said. "One man's word and a grainy video. Did you even see her face?"

"He said her name."

"Did you see her face?"

"No, but—"

"You saw what you wanted to see," Bianca said in disgust. "What your jealous eyes feared. You're a fool."

"Bianca," her uncle said in warning.

"Who is it?" Claude asked.

Broderick turned to Margaret.

Claude and Papa Bola stared at her dumbfounded when she fell on her knees and begged for forgiveness telling them all that she'd done. Her mother did no such thing and calmly watched her daughter with a detached expression.

Claude rushed over to Harmony and fell on his knees. "I'm so sorry. I didn't mean it. I—"

Harmony took a step back. "Get up. I forgive you," she said in a calm voice and he smiled in relief until she said, "but I'll never marry you."

"I'll make this up to you."

"You can do that by learning to trust."

Esther didn't pay attention to the young pair. Instead she stared at Ursula in confusion, not understanding why her sister had done what she had. "Why?"

"Why?" Ursula said with a sniff of disdain. "Because you humiliated me. You always have. Always will. I wanted you to feel the pain I've felt every day of my life."

"But I've always been good to you."

"It's easy to be good to a goat you're about to slaughter."

"I don't know what you mean."

"I'm sick of starving while you grow fat and rich. For just one day I wanted you to feel this hunger too. To feel helpless. To feel betrayed. To feel ashamed." She turned to Bianca. "And don't look so smug." She waved her finger between her and Broderick. "The love between you two is a lie. They're all behind it. Your dear, sweet cousin too."

Bianca turned to Harmony confused, but her cousin would not meet her gaze.

"Don't expect them to tell you anything," Ursula said. She looked at Broderick then cast her gaze over to Claude, Leonard and Papa Bola. "These three let you believe that she loved you." She turned her gaze to Esther and Harmony before she looked at Bianca. "And these two connived to make you think that he loved you. So no one should judge me for a deception I didn't begin."

"Harmony? Aunty?" Bianca said, her stomach churning with fear. "Is it true?"

Nobody spoke.

Broderick stood paralyzed trying to rationalize what he'd just heard. It had all been a lie? Then how come the previous day and night with her had felt so real? He saw the pain in her eyes and felt an acute sense of loss. But he wouldn't surrender to it; he had promised he wouldn't be the cause of her pain any longer. He didn't want to lose what they had and would fight to keep it. "It wasn't a deception," he said.

They all stared at him, but he kept his gaze on Bianca. "Remember when we first met in Italy?"

She nodded, her gaze unsure.

"And we escaped to a place where no one could see us?"

She hesitated.

"It was brief because we didn't want to be missed," he said quickly, hoping she would play along.

She blinked and finally understood, a slow smile touching her lips. "Yes," she said, taking a step towards him. "And I shared a mandarin with you."

He took a step towards her. "And a kiss."

She stopped a few feet away and looked up at him. "And I told you how I felt but you weren't ready."

He cupped her chin, his eyes melting into hers. "Oh, I was ready, but I wasn't eager to admit it yet." He took a deep breath, feeling the weight of what he was about to reveal, then touched his right ear. "And I didn't want you to know about this."

"Your partial deafness?" she said, saying the words he couldn't yet say, her warm gaze applauding his courage.

He nodded. "Yes, I didn't want anyone to know."

"So you ignored me the rest of the evening and I hated you for that," she said, filling in the story.

"And when I tried to explain later, you pushed me away and I hated you for that."

Her eyes shined up at him. "But you don't hate me anymore."

He smiled down at her. "I loved you then and I love you still. Always and forever," he said then turned their deception into something real by pulling her close and sealing his words with a kiss.

Chapter Twenty-five

"They are going to ruin everything!"

"Calm yourself, my dear. There's no need to be overexcited," Leonard said, watching his niece and her new husband walk down the aisle hand in hand. The ceremony, held at the Italian castle where they had first met, had been perfect, conducted outside in the breathtaking garden. By way of apology, Papa Bola had paid for the entire event including the extravagant reception that would soon follow. "They are now married."

"But the reception," Esther said concerned. "How can they have hired singers that nobody has ever heard of?"

"We've heard of her."

"A maid in our hotel," she said with a sigh. "What were they thinking? We must do something."

Harmony squeezed her mother's arm. "No, Mum. No one will interfere this time."

Fortunately, nobody had to. That evening, as the tiny lights lining the castle's panoramic terrace lit up like a golden crown against the lush green landscape and dark blue sky, the reception was just as perfect as the ceremony. Andrew and Miss Lovely sang a beautiful duet that left everyone in tears.

Aunt Ursula did not attend and her presence wasn't missed. Claude and Margaret did, neither yet ready to admit that their shared guilt had slowly blossomed into an affair.

Harmony danced and enjoyed herself feeling no pressure to marry until she was ready.

And Bianca and Broderick?

They danced together as husband and wife relieved their event had been without drama.

"Do you want to fly back to the States on my broomstick?" Bianca teased him.

Broderick shook his head. "My pet carrier is more comfortable," he said and then they laughed remembering the people they'd once been, still amazed by the people they'd become. Together they welcomed the future standing bright before them, knowing it would be filled with happiness and long-lasting, unwavering love.

Glossary

Ankara – a colorful cotton fabric primarily associated with Africa because of its patterns and motifs; commonly known as "African wax print"

Aso ebi – a uniform dress that is traditionally worn as show of solidarity during a major event such as wedding

Amala and edewu soup – Amala is a Nigerian food made out of yam or cassava flour. It is usually eaten with edewu soup, which is made out of edewu leaves.

Gele – is a large rectangular cloth tied on a woman's head in many different styles.

Ishin – Ackee, a tropical fruit.

English teacake – a light, sweet, yeast-based bun containing dried fruits, etc…

About the Author

Dara Girard is an award-winning, national bestselling author of more than thirty books including *Sweet Temptation, Midnight Promise, Unexpected Pleasure, Just One Look* and *The Amber Stone*. Dara loves to travel and hear from readers.

You can write her at:
contactdara@daragirard.com
or
P.O. Box 10345
Silver Spring, MD 20914

If you'd like to receive a reply, please send a self-addressed stamped envelope. Visit daragirard.com to join her newsletter and be the first to find out about current and upcoming releases.